"Ro...
Mi...

"Uh huh, and t... e
going to make i...

"That depends on us, doesn't it? On whether we're mature enough to live with each other's ideas and principles?"

"I was hoping to avoid all that."

"All what? Conflict? Roarke, if it wasn't a royal tomb it would be something else. No two people can live their lives together without some major clash."

"But clash over some despot's grave?" His eyes were angry, his smile gone. "No tomb," he hissed at her, "no matter who it belongs to, is worth people's lives."

HOPE McINTYRE

Hope McIntyre is the pseudonym for an author who lives in Sacramento, California, with her husband. She lived and worked in Korea with the U.S. Army and later received her master's degree in city planning, working as a planner on the East Coast before turning to fiction. Hope is a member of the Romance Writers of America and the National League of American Pen Women.

Hope McIntyre is a pseudonym for Ruth Barsten Tucker.

Dear Reader:

SILHOUETTE DESIRE is an exciting new line of contemporary romances from Silhouette Books. During the past year, many Silhouette readers have written in telling us what other types of stories they'd like to read from Silhouette, and we've kept these comments and suggestions in mind in developing SILHOUETTE DESIRE.

DESIREs feature all of the elements you like to see in a romance, plus a more sensual, provocative story. So if you want to experience all the excitement, passion and joy of falling in love, then SILHOUETTE DESIRE is for you.

Karen Solem
Editor-in-Chief
Silhouette Books

HOPE McINTYRE

Moon On East Mountain

Published by Silhouette Books New York
America's Publisher of Contemporary Romance

SILHOUETTE BOOKS, a Division of Simon & Schuster, Inc.
1230 Avenue of the Americas, New York, N.Y. 10020

Distributed by Pocket Books

ISBN: 0-671-52527-1

First Silhouette Books printing September, 1984

10 9 8 7 6 5 4 3 2 1

America's Publisher of Contemporary Romance

Printed in the U.S.A.

BC91

To my mother, Ramona Barsten, who taught me to reach for the stars

How many friends have I? Count them:
Water and stone, pine and bamboo—
The rising moon on the east mountain,
Welcome, it too is my friend.
What need is there, I say
To have more friends than five?

Yun Son Do,
17th century Korean poet

1

It was the beginning of spring in Korea.

Clover McBain let the warm, humid air move seductively through her hair as she stood on her fifth-floor office balcony. In a subconscious gesture she tugged at the neat chignon and shook her head so the red-golden curls fell free around her slender shoulders.

Whiffs of spice and garlic drying on the steep hillsides nearby drifted across to her and she breathed deeply, the fragrances enticing and exotic. It was this sense of the Oriental lands she loved so much—an aura that helped minimize her difficulties.

At the moment her difficulties seemed solvable, but her spirits were depressed. Why, after a particularly harsh winter, did the beauty of spring make her feel discordant? She tried to analyze her mood. Was it the job? City planning in any country was frustrating at best, but here in South Korea it seemed especially tiresome. She had the twentieth-century woman's need to get on with it, but she was working in a culture that meticulously observed ancient traditions, slowing everything to a snail's crawl.

Impatience, that was her problem, surely. After two years she should have been used to the Korean way of doing things.

Clover turned abruptly and walked back to her office to face the mound of work piled on her desk. She was, after all, sole proprietress of a joint Korean-American effort to redevelop the district of Yong Dong Pō, and as a principal of David Thompson and Associates she had arrived at the pinnacle of her profession. She had bid for and won a lucrative international planning contract awarded by the municipal government of Seoul.

Now, incredibly, the government had decided to put the second phase of her contract up for bid in spite of their earlier reassurances that her firm would be given the work. Hastily, she had drawn up bid papers and submitted them. She knew Thompson and Associates could as easily perform site preparation and engineering for the new town as plan it. So why the jitters? She waited, more than a little anxious, to hear from the mayor.

An irritating commotion in the hall outside the reception area jarred her. She supposed her advanced state of nervousness made her more vulnerable to annoyances than usual, so she tried to ignore the disturbance—without too much success.

Scraping noises of furniture being dragged and pushed along the corridor, the grinding creak of the ancient elevator door closing and then opening again, tempted her to rush headlong into the hall and vent her frustrations on whoever was out there.

A sonorous voice above the noise, much like a deep-toned temple bell, made Clover lift her head. It soothed the happy, noisy workers. No upper-class Korean would supervise a cacophonous venture like that, so who spoke with such velvet authority? Now she was openly curious,

tilting her head, straining to hear mor
intrigued her and sent her senses yearnin
puzzled frown crossed her face at the unspok
that rose and fell in waves, feelings she w
acknowledge. When the voice faded Clover
sense of loss.

She certainly did not expect her morning
stroyed by the sudden appearance in the doo
tall, swarthy American in blue jeans and open-n
shirt. She stared in amazement as he swaggered
office unannounced with a large white-toothed s
contrasted violently with his sun-darkened fa
piercing charcoal eyes. Her heart skipped severa
before she silently ordered it to be sensible. Unbel
she recognized Roarke Devereaux from his pictur

In a few long strides he was in front of her. He f
his lithe, muscular frame into a monk's chair, swu
heavy booted foot up on her desk, and said, "So, yo
Clover S. McBain! Somehow I expected a dried-u
lady with orthopedic shoes."

Still in a state of shock and unable to settle down
enough to speak coherently, her vivid green eyes
ened in anger at the arrogance of this man.

"I'm Roarke Devereaux, by the way," he finall
his voice ringing deep into her now distracted spiri
same voice that had penetrated her heart and min
moments ago.

Roarke made no attempt to hide his appraisal
Then he smiled in obvious satisfaction, a smile
assumed meant that she had the approval of
preme judge of women.

"What do you want, Mr. Devereaux?" she as
carefully controlled voice that belied her anxiety

"Tell me about our project," he answered.

Clover hesitated, confused. "Our what?"

"Project, Clover. I'm doing the site prep and

for Yong Dong Pō. Didn't you know? That was me
u heard moving into the offices down the hall." He
lined his head toward the door.

"I'm afraid I don't understand. Since when are you
orking on the Yong Dong Pō project? And would you
ind taking your foot off my desk?"

"Oh, the lady has spirit. I like that." He laughed. "I
on the Phase Two contract." His eyes studied her face
nd Clover felt waves of panic wash over her. "Sorry,
Clover, I thought you knew," he said as he moved his
oot from her desk.

"No, I didn't." She tried to keep her expression frozen but she was angry as feelings of betrayal welled up in her. Not to win the contract she felt was hers was one thing, but to find out from her competitor was too much to bear. She leaned slightly forward to face this man, who looked and acted more like a rogue Arab with his tightly curled black hair and craggy features than the upper-class Bostonian he reportedly was.

She had never met Roarke before today, although she knew he had worked as a civil engineer in Korea for several years. His reputation as a ruthless and aggressive businessman combined with the constant rumors linking him with beautiful women in and out of Korea, made her shudder.

Anger rose in her throat and she leaned even more toward Roarke, hoping to take control of the volatile situation as well as her own apprehension.

"Mr. Devereaux . . ."

His gaze was intense. "Call me Roarke," he said.

"Mr. Devereaux, if you please. I would greatly appreci-
te a little common courtesy from you. You come
ursting into my office, put your foot on my desk, and
nnounce that you are now my engineer—"

"Just a damned minute, Miss McBain. I am not *your*
ngineer. I am *the* engineer on the project. Devereaux

Enterprises is your partner. We don't work for each other, we work together. Understand? The reason I got the contract is because I have more engineering experience than you or your firm. Let's get that straight right now or the next few years will be pretty miserable for both of us."

Clover was shaking with impotent rage, realizing that her emotions and temper were fast getting the upper hand. "Please forgive me if I seem angry, because I am," she said as calmly as she could. "How dare you walk in here like you own the place? This is *my* planning project. You are here to prepare the site. Nothing more, nothing less."

As suddenly as he had burst into her office all smiles and goodwill, he darkened. The black curly hair encircling his beautifully masculine face seemed to bristle with anger.

Quietly he said, "Do you come on that strong with every man you meet? Why all the frustrated anger?"

Was he ridiculing her? "Mr. Devereaux . . ."

"Again, call me Roarke. Please. We're not supposed to be enemies."

The face of my adversary, she thought. Why does it have to be so damned attractive? His name stuck in her throat. "Roarke," she finally said. "I . . . uh . . . look, until this morning I was confident we had a good project going here. I've heard about you and your construction methods. Bulldoze everything down and start over. Not here in Yong Dong Pō, Mr. Engineer, or we will be enemies."

Roarke leaned toward Clover and took her chin gently in his hand. His strong body, with its scent of freshly scrubbed masculinity, overwhelmed her. His piercing black eyes sent an erotic message down her spine and probed her emotions like a hot poker. She pulled away, afraid he could hypnotize her.

She was certain Roarke knew she had bid on that contract and lost. Was he mocking her? Just what kind of a man was he?

Roarke continued the conversation in spite of Clover's enmity. "Just remember, I'm the engineer. When I say something has to go, that's it, lady!" He sat down again, grim and hard.

"Who do you think you are to tell me that when you make a decision the world must abide by it? Neither of us has the final word. Prince Yee and his advisory committee are our liaison to city hall. They and the government make the final decisions. This isn't some poor, third-world country, as you should know. We aren't the all-knowing Americans, telling them what to do. We work for them and they make the decisions."

"Well, thank you for the lecture, but I've been in this country a lot longer than you have. I know the people and I'm fully aware of who we work for."

"Good for you, Mr. Devereaux."

"Look, why don't you tell me what the Yee committee wants, and knock off the hostility."

Clover swallowed hard and fought the urge to argue with him further. She believed he simply didn't understand his place in the scheme. At least he was aware that there was a committee that had the right to veto any decision. She folded her hands on the desk, desperately trying to keep her mind on the project and off the man who sat draped over her monk's chair in apparent ease, as if the world did indeed belong to him and did do his bidding.

She took a deep breath, put on her best businesslike face, and spoke in as composed a manner as this topsy-turvy morning would allow. "Next week we have to begin clearing several blocks of old wooden structures in order to build housing for the river-dwellers. You're aware of the problem, I'm sure."

"Yes. I've already looked the buildings over. There's no chance of saving them. They're too dilapidated."

"We're all aware of that," she cut him off abruptly. "The committee has mapped out the entire plan. The first phase, as you know, is to create a new neighborhood, complete with stores, temples, churches, meeting places, parks, and apartments that simulate the close-knit ties the river people have formed over the years."

"How do they feel about it?"

"The river people? After Prince Yee talked to them, they agreed to move peacefully. Their Baptist minister, the Reverend Cho, is on the committee and he reviews all of the plans." Roarke raised an eyebrow, but Clover couldn't tell if he was impressed or contemptuous. "Anyway, the idea is to transplant not only the people, but their traditions, friends, neighbors, and religious leaders. I'm grateful that Prince Yee is the chairman. His reputation and the respect everyone has for him make his support valuable beyond measure."

"Isn't he American-educated? MIT or something?" Roarke asked.

Clover was surprised that Roarke didn't know more about the Prince. "Yes. He's an American citizen educated at MIT in architecture. By the way, he's also an engineer," she said, waiting for a reaction from Roarke.

"Oh," was all he said.

Clover smiled. At least one person would be able to evaluate Roarke's decisions and keep him in line.

"Sounds like a good beginning. What's the next step?" he asked.

"The next steps are in yellow on the map." Clover pointed to a large multicolored map on the wall behind her drafting table. "We'll rehabilitate most of the district rather than tear it down; that is, if we have your permission."

"No need to get sarcastic. I'm not totally insensitive to planning and rehab."

"How nice," she replied.

Roarke flashed a broad smile at her like a beacon light. "I think it would be a good idea if we called a truce and tried to be friends," he said. "We have two years to butt heads or work together peacefully."

He was right. In spite of the antagonism and in spite of the dangerous sexual attraction underlying their bickering, they must somehow get along in order to complete the contracts.

"We're friends, then." Clover tried to give Roarke a sincere smile but her face felt tight. She knew she had to meet this man on equal terms and show her equanimity, or what was left of it. She finally managed to smile at him.

"Good! Now what shall we do this weekend?"

"What?" Clover asked weakly.

"This weekend. Let's go pheasant-hunting on Cheju Dō."

Clover was speechless. She had never encountered a man like Roarke Devereaux.

"Sorry, but I'm busy this weekend."

Roarke, although he did not change his expression, stopped for a moment. "Ah?"

Clover thought she detected a tilt of his high and mighty cheekbones, a tilt that said he wasn't used to being turned down—by anyone.

"Yes."

"I see. Perhaps next weekend? The weather'll be perfect for a month or so."

"I'm booked for a few years," she replied.

He grinned and stood up. "Okay, Skoshi, I'll play your game for a while but Cheju Dō is really a nice spot for getting acquainted. I have a little house there and it's very cozy."

Clover grinned back. At well over six feet, Roarke could see her as "Skoshi," or petite. Not many men saw as small the tall, willowy frame that she had hated since she was a teenager growing up in a small community south of San Francisco. It amused her, and his bright smile enticed her just as his voice had in the hall a while ago. How long could she hold back from him, from his overwhelming sexual charm that he used like a sledgehammer?

But Clover stopped short of encouraging him. She had heard about Roarke's cozy spots and his reputation with women. Charm them, master them, seduce them, and go on to the next challenge.

"No thanks, Roarke. I think you'll have to find someone else to play games with."

Roarke laughed and waved good-bye as he backed out of her office.

Clover bit her lower lip, partly in anger and partly because of a sensation she could not define. She hadn't felt attracted to a man since her husband died, only six months after they were married. That was four years ago and she was constantly on guard, holding her heart and her susceptibilities in check lest they get out of hand and she lose her head over another adventurous man who cared nothing about the consequences of his actions.

John McBain had been a race car driver and all of her pleadings had failed to keep him off the track. He died a man possessed, burned in a flaming wreckage at Daytona. Clover was in the pit when his car flipped over in front of her, careened into a wall, and burst into flames. It was a blackened shell before the rescue squads could reach it. The numbness she felt from the tragedy, and by the years of nightmares reliving the crash over and over again until she was afraid to go to sleep at night, made her almost contentious toward other men.

Now that she had managed to make a life for herself, the nightmares had subsided to a sickening memory, and she vowed never again to experience the kind of hurt she had had with John and his recklessness.

She sat down at her desk, unable to further concentrate on the work before her, vaguely dissatisfied with herself for overreacting to the handsome and bewildering Roarke Devereaux. He stirred in her almost every negative feeling she was capable of—anger, hate, fear, indignation—and even desire.

She must have had a terrifying expression on her face when her exuberant secretary, Betty Witherspoon, came into her office. "Boy, you look upset! What is it?" the secretary asked.

"Didn't you see that man?"

"You mean the one backing out of your office a few minutes ago?"

"Yes."

"I was away from my desk when he came in. Isn't that the notorious Roarke Devereaux? I've seen his pictures in the paper."

"Oh, Betty, it was, and he came in to tell me he won the Phase Two contract." Clover's voice was unbelieving. "How could they? I had Prince Yee's advisory committee behind me. It was logical for me to get that contract. They know my work, Betty. We've done a good job this last year. So why didn't I get it?"

"Perhaps they thought the engineering phase would be more suited to Roarke Devereaux. After all, they know his work, too. He just finished a dam on the Soyang River," Betty reminded her gently.

"Dam?" Clover gave Betty a venomous look. "He's only a public works engineer—with all the sensitivity that goes with it. Why would they think he can do a suburban rehabilitation project? That's stupid. That's . . . that's . . . Oh, damn Roarke Devereaux!"

A feeling of betrayal overpowered her. Roarke had stolen that contract from her and she would be forced to work with him for the next two years.

After a moment of reflection, her natural competitive drive, a will to pick up any challenge, began to surface. Roarke Devereaux might be the biggest challenge of her life, but she would look forward to a confrontation with him. She smiled, almost enjoying a perverted need to give him a run for his New England dollar. And, by God, she would.

". . . Clover? Are you listening?" Betty's voice broke through Clover's angry thoughts.

"What?"

"I was saying that it seems to me that he's just about the sexiest man I've seen in years. Don't you think?"

"No, I don't! He's every bit the S.O.B. I'd imagined he'd be. Now Betty, don't get that gleam in your eyes again. I've had enough of your matchmaking, thank you."

"Hmmm." Betty picked up papers from Clover's out box, and as she walked away she said, "Just don't pass up any good opportunities. Devereaux's not only sexy, but rich too, I hear."

"A rounder, you might add," Clover mumbled.

"So much more to make them interesting," she answered, walking out of the office.

Clover shook her head. That was all she needed. Betty Witherspoon, older and wiser than Clover, widowed also, was the perpetual matchmaker. Clover didn't need encouragement where Roarke was concerned, but help in fending him off.

Just then the round, adorable face of Clover's seven-year-old paper boy peered through the open door, eager and full of anticipation.

"Hello, Clover!" he said.

Her animosity immediately disappeared. "Hello, Myune," she said, and gestured for him to come in all the way. "Sit down and tell me about your excursion yesterday."

The small waif walked over and perched on the same monk's chair that Roarke had abandoned minutes before.

"I see things," he began, but his eyes and attention drifted quickly from her face to the candy jar on her desk.

"Would you like some candy?" she asked. He nodded his head and reached for the jar. "Well? What happened and what did you see?"

"Things," he repeated.

Exasperated, she prodded him. "What things, Myune?"

"A tomb where old people were buried a long time ago. It was scary." He giggled.

"That was the royal tomb at Uijongbu. I hope you listened to your teacher explain why it was important."

Myune lowered his head. "I was scared of ghosts," he admitted.

Clover wanted to laugh, but Myune was so serious that she stifled a smile and said, "Well, never mind. Would you like to go to another this weekend? It's just being excavated. I'll take you along with me."

His eyes brightened and he nodded solemnly. Excursions with Clover meant she would buy something for him and bring along a basket filled with food and sweets.

"Okay, chum. Give me my paper and hurry along. Don't be late for school."

Myune handed the paper to her and skipped away through the door.

After Myune left, Clover felt more at ease with herself. It was still early for lunch but she decided to take a break from the office anyway. Eager to be away from the building, she walked briskly down the hall to the stairway, opened the door, and ran down the stairs. She rounded the third-floor landing as Roarke was coming up with a box of books in his hands. He set the box down to block her way.

"Now," he said, "shall we try all over again as if I didn't charge into your office and put my boot on your pretty desk?"

"I'm sorry I was hostile, but I'm sure you understand how I felt about that contract. Usually I can control my temper. Will you shake hands and agree to be a friendly business associate?" she asked, holding out her slender, well-manicured hand.

"I'll shake, but for being close friends as well," he answered, shaking her hand slowly, then raising it to his lips, planting light tingling kisses on her fingertips.

"Roarke, I can't respond to men coming on with advances that smack of one-night stands. Maybe someday we can hunt on Cheju Dō, but I have to get to know you better. Please," she said, pulling her hand away, "don't push me." She knew her voice was trembling, but she could do nothing to stop it.

He leaned against the wall and folded his arms. "I guess I've been knocking around the world too long. Life for me is the here and now. This job will be the first one I have had that will keep me settled for more than a few months in one place. Maybe I have a lot to learn, too. Okay. We'll get to know each other a few weeks before I press my invitation again." His eyes danced seductively. He bent over and retrieved his box and walked up the stairs. His jeans were tight, revealing firm muscular thighs and a flat, handsome bottom. Clover caught herself staring at him as he took the stairs three at a time. Mesmerized by the retreating backside, she shook off the desire to run after him, to hear his voice, to see him walk away again.

The goose bumps on her arms disappeared as she ran headlong down the stairs, out the first-floor exit, and onto the busy street that led to the beach along the Han River.

The street called Han Way led in an unerring line to the Han River—the source of life in Seoul, Korea. Like the Nile in Egypt, it crested and receded year after year, leaving a thick brown silt behind. But unlike the Nile people, Koreans did not use the silt to refresh their fields. And now the flooding, although diminished by dams upriver, merely served as a gross inconvenience to the city and a danger to the squatters who lived in rice-thatched huts along the banks. But the Han nevertheless was a symbol of life, and in the days of war served as a temporary barrier to invading armies as well.

Today Clover wanted solace, and only the slow-moving Han could give it to her. She sometimes frequented a small beach that lay hidden near the main bridge into Seoul, picking her way over the slippery rocks to find a spot in the shade to sit and think. Here, the sounds of the city could not be heard because of the bubble of water battering its way over rocks and around the bridge pylons, drowning out all but her own thoughts.

And her thoughts were on Roarke Devereaux. Why, of all the men she had met in the last four years, did *he* make her blood boil?

For an instant she was angry, but anger quickly melted away. Roarke Devereaux had possessed her with his eyes and she was frightened and unsure of herself—a feeling that had become alien to her.

She passed Mr. Yun's shop on the way to the river and walked in. The heady, almost giddy feeling she could not control must have shown. Mr. Yun looked startled as she picked up a piece of dried squid and plunked it down on the counter.

"You want *that,* Young Ni?" he asked.

"Uh-huh," she laughed. "My midmorning snack."

Mr. Yun shook his head, not taking his eyes from her. "Three hundred sixty won," he said.

She gave him the money.

"You okay?" he asked, perplexed.

"Of course I am."

"Not like Young Ni," he mumbled as he put the money in his apron pocket.

The nickname the Koreans had given her still baffled her. Young Ni, translated literally, meant "beautiful valley." But Clover didn't press the point, and accepted the name without asking questions she might not want the answers to.

She made her way through the crowds, moving in an

endless procession over the gray-brick sidewalks, passing open shops with dirt floors, dodging farmers with carts pulled by yellow oxen. In this enclave of old Korea, untouched by the drastic modernization of the rest of Seoul, she saw, felt, touched, and smelled what Korea must have been like just after the Second World War and again after the Korean War. People struggling to make a living any way they could. Men who gathered the night soil to sell to rice farmers, women carrying enormous bundles of rags on their heads, and a sea of humanity working with primitive tools, making just enough money each day to buy food and pay for their meager shelter. How did one preserve the good in all of this and still raise the standard of living for them? It was a delicate balance that Clover knew had to be maintained. And Prince Yee and his committee would have to be the force to make it all work.

Clover knew she had to come to terms with Roarke Devereaux if she was to be effective. She wanted the peace the Han River could give her as a respite from the restless mood Roarke had put her in. But Roarke had made something snap within her and peace no longer seemed possible. Turbulence had replaced the inner quietude she had worked so hard to find. She breathed deeply, as her yoga master had taught her, but it was useless. Her feelings reminded her of the turmoil she had fought after John's death—restless, unyielding, demanding. Only now it was Roarke's face she saw, not John's.

2

On Saturday morning Clover gathered up Myune from his hovel on the outskirts of Yong Dong Pō and from the cackling old woman who claimed to be a distant cousin of his dead mother. Mrs. Kaeng was a charwoman at the local cement plant—probably the worst job anyone could have, so Clover bore her complaints and ravings with sympathy.

The room the old woman shared with Myune had no windows; the hut was made of scrap corrugated steel, discarded boards, and wattle carelessly stuffed in cracks to keep out the winds. The door was nailed boards of all sizes, held together with rusty hinges of different types so that the entire effect from a distance was one of a box whose sides and front sat catywampus on a steep hillside.

Clover wanted to find them a place to live that would be suitable, but she had been warned away by a friend, Doctor Lee, who said that the Koreans preferred Americans not to interfere in their daily lives, even to the extent those lives were improved. So Clover took Myune away from the hut and the random care inflicted by the old woman as much as possible, gave him clothes and bedding to make him comfortable, and paid for his schooling in a private academy.

She slipped a handful of won to the old lady to quiet her, and took Myune away. They hurried down streets still damp from the early-morning mist that lay across the land, giving it the old name (Chosen—Land of Morning Calm). Both Clover and Myune were used to early hours and were happy to get started before the sun was high enough to burn off the fog.

Before they drove to the countryside, Clover stopped by the office. As she sat at her desk working on a troublesome letter to David Thompson, the head of her firm, she felt the presence again—Roarke Devereaux. She cursed his name under her breath, but continued to draft the letter, searching for the right words to tell David that she did not get the Phase II contract. Clover knew she had somehow let David down, and was angry with herself for allowing Roarke Devereaux to upstage her.

Myune stiffened and stopped munching on a piece of candy, staring wide-eyed at the door. Without a sound, like a cooling breeze, Roarke appeared and leaned against the jamb, arms akimbo, his eyes watching her from under heavy black eyebrows, a frown of mock concern on his face. Beside him a large German shepherd stood like a sentinel, ears alert. He smiled. "So this is my rival." He looked at Myune.

"Hardly, Roarke," Clover said, not smiling. "This is Myune. Myune, this is Mr. Devereaux. He has the office down the hall and will work with me on the project."

Myune smiled, keeping his eyes on the dog. Then he asked shyly, "You want a newspaper?"

"Myune!" she admonished. "Don't be forward."

"You sell newspapers?"

"Uh-huh. I deliver in the morning before school. Clover say I have to go to school. We went to a tomb this week. It was scary."

"Well, then, I expect to start the paper Monday morning. That okay with you, Myune?" Roarke asked.

"Uh-huh." The boy grinned.

"Pay him ahead of time, Roarke. Myune has to buy his papers before he gets them to deliver. It's sixty-eight hundred won a year."

"Yes, ma'am." Roarke saluted Clover, dug into his pocket, pulled out the money, and gave it to Myune. "Here you go."

"Thank you," Myune said, looking at Clover for approval.

She smiled and went back to her letter.

"Where are you going today, Myune?" Roarke asked.

"For a picnic in the countryside. Clover look at tomb and I'll play and eat. You want to go?" Myune asked before Clover could stop him.

And before Clover could stop Roarke, he said, "Sure, I'd love to. Where's your picnic basket?"

"Mr. Yun." Myune pointed in the direction of Mr. Yun's shop.

"Hey, why don't we go over and get it while Clover finishes her work, huh, pal?" Roarke asked.

"It's all paid for and waiting. I'll be finished in a minute," Clover said.

"Myune and I will do the honors and come back for you." Roarke ignored the frown on her face.

She watched him take Myune's hand and leave her office without so much as a glance her way. The dog followed, limping.

Still vibrating from Roarke's sudden appearance, she stared at the empty doorway. She felt a momentary stab of regret over her decision to reject him, but it had to be. A shadow of uncertainty crossed her face as she realized just how difficult her life would be now that he had stirred her heart and awakened sleeping desires. How simple her life had been until Roarke walked into her office.

Clover found herself waiting for Roarke and Myune to return, glancing up from her letter to David at the merest noise in the hall. Finally, she heard Myune's laughter echo in the hall. She heard another laugh, one of a man enjoying himself in innocent fun with a child, and her heart once again twisted in her tightened chest. She would never have suspected Roarke to have a genuine, warm laugh that was as welcoming as the morning sun, and it warmed her momentarily, until she remembered it was the same Roarke Devereaux who had marched into her office, put his foot on her desk, and declared himself the engineer whose word was law. Roarke Devereaux be damned!

Roarke and Myune walked into her office laughing about some secret, and, to her amazement, plopped a huge picnic basket, twice the size of the one she had ordered, onto her desk.

"You should see the stuff Roarke bought," Myune cried. "I can't wait until we eat!"

"Mr. Devereaux, Myune," she corrected gently.

"No. He said I can call him Roarke. Can't I, Clover?" he pleaded.

Clover looked up at Roarke and gave him a disapproving look. "If that's what he wants, you can." She tried to make her voice cold to impress upon Roarke that she did not like the familiarity.

"Okay. Can we go now?" Myune asked. "Roarke has a funny truck we're going in. It's high, so I can see out of it and over all the people in the streets."

"I thought we were going in my car. My, but you do take over, don't you Mr. Devereaux?"

His grin told her all she needed to know. He *would* take over and she had better watch out.

* * *

They bounced and jolted along the streets of Yong Dong Pō with Myune and the dog, Samantha, in the back seat. Myune excitedly pointed to this and that along the way, shouting his comments from his exalted position in the back seat of Roarke's Land Rover.

"Myune, why don't you quiet down, please?" Clover said.

"Okay," the compliant little boy answered. But his eyes were wide with pleasure as he peered out of one side then another. Clover turned to Roarke and studied him.

After a moment, he turned his head toward her and asked, "Well, do I suit you?"

"Roarke, we're business associates. Why must you drag that fact down to the level of whether or not you suit me or vice versa? I don't know if you 'suit' me or not until I see what kind of work you do."

He smiled. "You're a beautiful woman—trim, chic, and desirable. How the hell do you expect me to think of you in strictly professional terms? I know you do good work. I've seen the village at Pusan. In fact, I'm willing to concede you do brilliant work. If I had known you were gorgeous, too, I'd have made it a point to meet you sooner."

"To what end?" She immediately regretted asking the question, and continued, "So I do brilliant work. Can't you just think of me that way?"

"The end is mine to know, and yes, I like intelligent women. Simpering fluffs just don't make it. I like my women tough, independent, and spirited. That way we can make love and part friends without the silly romantic nonsense most women expect."

"For heaven's sake," Clover hissed. "Myune's in the back seat. Keep your comments less candid."

She looked back at Myune, who appeared to be absorbed with the scenery and Sam the dog—not in their conversation.

"I agree. We'll discuss sweet nothings when Myune goes off to play and leaves us to get acquainted," he whispered back.

"There won't be time for that. Sorry. We're going to a new excavation of another royal tomb. I plan to spend time looking at it. You'll have to make do with the sun and water."

"We'll see," he said.

Roarke turned the Land Rover south on a newly widened and paved highway for an hour's drive to Suwon, a major city on the west coast of South Korea. At Suwon they turned onto a two-lane road and headed southwest to Paranjang, a village nestled on a hillside facing the Yellow Sea. Here, where the small valley was sandwiched between the hills and sea, a farmer had unexpectedly stumbled across a tomb, possibly that of a prince or minor royal sibling.

It was nine in the morning and the sun had long since burned off the fog as the Land Rover rounded the last curve on the hilly coastal road. Roarke pulled over and stopped.

"I know the men who fought here during the war and maybe some who were stationed here in the decade after would think me crazy, but Korea is one of the most beautiful countries in the world," Roarke said softly.

Clover nodded. She didn't expect softness from Roarke. He was too macho, too rugged, to claim anything but gruff acceptance of his surroundings.

They surveyed the valley below in silence. It was peaceful, pastoral, and unbidding—qualities fast dying out in Korea. This was how it was a thousand years ago.

Roarke started the Land Rover when he spotted a car coming down the hill behind them. They rode the rest of the way in silence, delighting in the beauty that unfolded before them.

"It's beautiful, isn't it?" Roarke said.

"Yes, it is." Clover wondered how he could appreciate beauty one moment and destroy it with his bulldozers the next. She just didn't understand a man with such conflicting sensibilities.

The steep descent into the Paranjang Valley ended at the edge of the village. Roarke parked the Land Rover under a tree, took the enormous picnic basket out, and helped Myune down from the car. Clover, Roarke, and Myune, holding Sam, trailed one behind the other along a narrow path that led through the ancient village.

Korea in its early spring beauty stood before them. Pristine black pines jutted out of the hills, silhouetted against the aqua-blue of the sea, white, glistening beaches spread out beyond, interrupted by outcroppings of granite rock.

"Look, Roarke." Clover tugged at his sleeve. He put his hand on her elbow to steady her as she aimed her camera at the picturesque view ahead. She hesitated a few seconds longer than needed to adjust her settings, letting Roarke's hand linger on her arm.

A symmetry of green and blue outlined the rice paddies and the verdant grasses that had already begun sprouting after a harsh winter. The L-shaped, rice-thatched roofs of the traditional Korean houses snuggled together at one end of the extensive paddies. Wisps of smoke from wood fires filtered through the air, and Clover breathed deeply to catch the fragrance.

Around the corner of a house ahead, two women emerged balancing baskets of laundry on their heads. Laughing and talking in their high musical voices, they stopped to stare at the strange entourage. Roarke and Clover stood heads higher than the laundry baskets, like looming giants over the tiny women. Tourists were rare in this remote area, so a long eye contact was made. Then the women cupped their hands over their mouths to suppress giggles of embarrassment, and began to walk around the newcomers.

Roarke bowed and spoke Korean to the women, whose obvious amazement was reflected in their weathered faces. The women fled the scene, too shy to strike up a conversation.

Clover could hear them discussing the encounter in fast-clipped, excited voices as they hurried away toward the communal wash well at the other end of the town.

"That'll give them something to talk about for a week," Roarke said, laughing.

"Your Korean is beautiful. Perfect inflection," Clover called to Roarke's back as they kept up a fast pace along the path. When they had cleared the village they stopped at the edge of the rice paddies. Roarke pulled Clover up on a check separating the crescent-shaped fields flooded and bursting with green rice shoots.

"We'll have to cross on the checks or else walk completely around them over there. Game for tippy-toeing through the paddies with me?"

"Sure. How about you, Myune? Want to walk along the checks?"

"Okay, let's go. Come, Sam," the boy called to the dog. The lame dog humped along eagerly.

"Myune first, so I can watch him," Roarke called. "Come on Sam, you next."

"I'll come last," Clover shouted.

"The water's not deep, but if you fall in, it's messy!" Roarke laughed.

"I'm well aware of the consequences," she called back. Night soil, human excrement, was still used in fertilizing small family rice paddies, and the smell was powerful. To fall in would be devastating!

Clover watched Myune and Roarke walk gingerly along the low narrow levee separating the paddies, tiered one below the other to facilitate flooding. She followed, having as much fun in this game of "keep-your-balance" as Myune was.

Curious faces looked up from the men and women tending the paddies, their backs seemingly forever bent in the never-ending process of transplanting rice seedlings, later to tend them and then harvest the Oriental staple in summer. Roarke called greetings to the workers and they responded good-naturedly.

Clover loved the spontaneous Koreans—never suspicious, only curious about Americans, and doubly so when they could communicate with the foreigners. Shouts of encouragement rose from the men who watched the procession cross their fields. It would never occur to them to challenge the strange invaders or keep them off the land.

"Clover, look." Roarke said, pointing to their right. A farmer was plowing a paddy with a yellow ox, using the same type of crude wood plow his ancestors used hundreds, even thousands, of years before. It churned the muddy silt and mixed in the night soil so the paddy could be flooded later and more rice planted. Roarke reached back to steady her; his touch reassured her, and she took her time to frame the scene in her camera lens.

"This is the nicest outing we've had this year," Clover said.

"For me, too," Myune shouted.

When they had reached the far side of the rice fields, Clover directed Roarke toward the excavation, located in a gap in the mountains at the southern end of the valley. As they neared the site they could hear the high sing-song cries of workers hauling out the dirt in wicker baskets balanced on their heads. The sinewy men and women, toiling to uncover Korea's past, half ran and half walked along a narrow path and dumped the dirt into a huge bin covered with a wire mesh that caught any small artifact which might have escaped the attention of the students at the site. Another student sifted through the dirt with the intensity of a doctor performing delicate surgery.

Myune broke from Clover and Roarke and ran with the gimpy Sam along a path toward the sea. A Korean man in khaki fatigues waved to the two Americans. Clover pushed Roarke forward.

"Hello, Jin-Soo. Nice to see you. How's it going?" Clover shouted to the tall, handsome Korean who directed the dig.

"Fine, Clover. We have made significant progress."

"This is Roarke Devereaux, Jin-Soo. Roarke, this is Doctor Lee, Professor of Archaeology at the University."

"Ah, Mr. Devereaux," Jin-Soo said. "I have heard about you. Welcome to our dig." His face became masklike.

Clover cringed. She bet Jin-Soo Lee *had* heard about Roarke. After all, a tomb near Chunchon had been smothered forever beneath his bulldozers.

"Nice to meet you, Doctor. What do you hope to find here?" Roarke asked.

"I don't know. It's apparently a minor tomb, but one never knows until one looks."

Score one for Jin-Soo, Clover thought. "Do you mind if we just poke around?" she said aloud.

"Of course not. Please make yourselves comfortable. We have tea on the table over there."

"Thank you, but please don't worry about us. We brought a basket." Clover smiled as she gave Roarke a small shove to move him away from the archaeologist.

"Myune, please be careful," Clover called after the boy.

"Okay," Myune shouted back.

Roarke and Clover picked their way between students huddled in the dirt and brushing away a thousand years of grime from the granite blocks that marked the entrance to the tomb. Roarke was quiet as he watched the activity, his thoughts mirrored in his eyes.

"Won't you share them with me?" Clover asked.

"Share what?" He looked at her, his face questioning.

"Your thoughts. I can see them bouncing around in your head."

"I was just thinking what a waste of time this is. They've found almost twenty royal tombs in South Korea and brought up so much stuff they haven't even been able to catalogue it yet. All this energy and concentration could be better spent to enhance Korea's future rather than worry about a moldy prince who probably was a tyrant anyway."

"I see you are not in sympathy with our cultural heritage, Mr. Devereaux." Jin-Soo's voice startled them as he approached from behind.

"I think you need to expend more energy on your future, that's all." Roarke replied without emotion or hostility in his voice.

"You are wrong to deny us our past. It is easy for you to criticize our digs. Your New England past is chronicled in detail, so you take it for granted. We must dig deep, literally, to uncover our past."

"I don't care about my New England past. That's why I left."

"Pity." Jin-Soo's eyes narrowed as he studied Roarke. "What good is your noble commitment to a future without a past? Where is the ballast to steady your ship? The past gives us a foundation on which to build the future."

"I don't wish to argue with you, Doctor Lee. You have your beliefs and I have mine." Roarke began to walk away but Jin-Soo would not let him make light of Korea's heritage.

"When your actions affect my country, I do not believe you can be so indifferent."

Clover's heart raced as Roarke turned to face Jin-Soo. The archaeologist was a close friend of hers, but she had to work with Roarke. A nasty confrontation between them was something she couldn't afford. She resented Roarke's inviting himself along, but she had hoped his coming here would soften his recalcitrant attitude, not harden it.

"I don't think Roarke is indifferent. He just doesn't understand, Jin-Soo," Clover said.

"I don't need to have you apologize for me," Roarke snapped at Clover. "I think Doctor Lee and I both have valid opinions. I realize archaeology is his life. Building the future is mine." Roarke glared at Clover.

"I do not think," Jin-Soo Lee went on, still looking directly at Roarke, "that we will ever see it the same way—eye-to-eye, as you Americans say. But tell me, Mr. Devereaux, why are you so hostile to the past? I would be interested to know. Please, sit down and take tea with me. Let us talk of this matter." Doctor Lee offered Roarke and Clover small glasses of iced tea and gestured for them to sit in two canvas chairs around a card table littered with shards of pottery and small bones.

Roarke, polite but unmoved, sat down facing Lee. "Call me Roarke. May I call you Jin-Soo?" Roarke was offering a peace branch, which Lee seemed to accept.

"I prefer J.S. I got that name when I attended the California Institute of Technology."

"CIT?" Roarke's eyebrows shot up and his eyes widened. "That's my alma mater!"

"I see. Well, we must be friends, then. I find few people here who have gone to CIT. I'm an engineer by education as well as an archaeologist."

Clover burst out laughing. "That's marvelous! Roarke thinks only engineers have valid opinions. You never told me you're an engineer, Jin-Soo."

"Perhaps because my fervent interest lies in archaeology." He looked long at Clover, his face inscrutable. Roarke slowly moved his eyes from Lee to Clover and back.

"I wish our friend Clover S. McBain would alter her

stereotyped ideas about engineers. I do listen on occasion to planners and archaeologists," Roarke said sourly.

Doctor Lee smiled back at Clover and winked. His urbane face failed to register an expression, but Clover knew he was deeply concerned. "I understand you are now the engineer on the Yong Dong Pō project. I must congratulate you—the competition was stiff."

The jab hit home gently but effectively and Roarke again turned cool, sipping the iced tea, polite and indifferent.

Jin-Soo spoke quietly of his philosophy on Korea's past, and Clover thought she detected Roarke's hostility when Jin-Soo mentioned New England again. Apparently there was something in Roarke's past that made him recoil like a wounded panther. Clover tucked that information away for future use.

She couldn't continue to sit between these two proud, obstinate men while they took gentlemanly potshots at each other. She stood abruptly and started to walk away. "Jin-Soo is busy, Roarke. Shall we look around ourselves, and let him get back to the dig?"

"The lady's breaking it up," Roarke said.

The sarcasm irritated her. She turned to Jin-Soo. "Will I see you in class Wednesday evening?"

"Most assuredly, Clover. Perhaps dinner first?"

"I'd love it. We'll talk before then." Clover pulled Roarke with her as she hurried down a trail cut in the hillside and breathed a deep gulp of sea air to clear her mind.

Roarke was sullen and Clover couldn't decipher his thoughts. He grunted at her running commentary on the dig and showed a remarkable lack of enthusiasm until she suggested they walk down to the beach. She couldn't stand the unspoken tension between them.

Myune had already put his bathing suit on, but upon testing the water he decided it was too cold and scrounged the beach for shells. After spreading out a blanket, Clover sat down, legs folded under her, pretending an intense interest in the sea.

Roarke laid back with his hand clasped behind his head and closed his eyes. "I haven't relaxed like this for a year. Do you know this is the first day I haven't either worked or moved my office and equipment somewhere?"

Clover turned to him. "Since I met Myune, I've had lots of nice days relaxing or driving around Korea. He'd never left Yong Dong Pō and had no idea what the rest of his country was like. So I showed it to him. He's bright and a pleasure to be with."

"He's a cute kid," Roarke said with a faraway look in his eyes. "Tell me, Miss McBain," he asked suddenly, turning over on his stomach and propping himself on his elbows, "why aren't you married?"

"I am—it's Mrs. McBain," she replied with a perverse feeling of pleasure in teasing him.

He sat up with a start. "Married?" he choked out. "You are? Why haven't I heard?" The last sentence was spoken as if it had been his God-given right to be informed of such important matters.

She looked at him and was sorry she had teased him. His face reflected genuine concern.

"I'm a widow. I thought you knew."

"No, I didn't. Sorry." Roarke lay back again and took a deep breath.

"Would it have mattered?" She tipped her chin up in a gesture of defiance.

"Yes. I don't need that kind of problem."

"Oh? I thought perhaps it would eliminate another."

"Like what." He turned to her with a puzzled frown.

"Nothing."

"Like women falling in love? Married women certainly aren't immune to that. That's when the complications begin."

"Single women fall in love, too, Roarke."

He stared at her, his eyes seeming to penetrate the facade she had put on to avoid appearing vulnerable. Then he laughed—a loud, guffawing, shouting laugh that insulted her.

She started at the sound, not believing she had uttered those words about love and single women. She placed the palm of her hand against her face to cool off her tipsy emotions.

Roarke said, still laughing, "Blushing becomes you."

"I'm not blushing," she protested.

"When did he die?" Roarke was serious, as if he sensed Clover's hurt.

"A long time ago."

"So you're gun-shy."

"Yes. I guess I am."

Clover was close to Roarke, her shoulder touching his. A masculine scent caressed her nostrils and disappeared. He reached over and took her hand in his, squeezing it with a gentle sympathy, reassuring her. She felt buoyed by his apparent understanding—or was he apologizing for his callous laughter?

She liked the feel of his hard thigh against hers. The clear blue skies gradually clouded over and a cool breeze sent shivers through her. Roarke drew her closer to his side and the warmth of his body felt good.

Conflicting emotions disturbed Clover's temporary complacency. She wanted, almost desperately, to forget John McBain and begin to live again. Could she set aside her enormous and, as her mother had accused, unreasonable, guilt? But no one, including her mother, knew the full extent of her guilt and the circumstances surrounding John's death. It had all been her fault.

Would Roarke take her tattered emotions and mend them? Or would he use her, discard her, and leave the open wounds just as they were now? Roarke was a loner and she was lonely. God, what a terrible combination—ripe for all sorts of complications.

"Now it's your turn," he said.

"To do what?"

"Share your thoughts," he answered in a soft voice that made Clover want to turn and pour her heart out to him—the long years of forgetting, the loneliness, the ache when she went to bed at night by herself, remembering John's warm caresses and soft sweet words of love, the nightmares, the anger, and the bitterness, too—all there to mix with the memories of her past.

"I've discovered something I hadn't counted on, and I can't trust you with it."

"Just what the hell do you think you know about me? We only met yesterday. Boy, you really judge a man harshly without knowing a damn thing about him."

"I know your reputation, Roarke."

"Well, I know yours, too. But I was prepared to judge you on your merits, not on gossip. I don't suppose you realize they call you the cold mountain?" he blurted out.

"Young Ni? It means beautiful valley."

"The hell it does. The mountains surrounding Seoul are the most beautiful when they're covered with snow. But they're cold as death. Young Ni means beautiful *above* the valley. The cold mountains."

Clover froze. Tears welled up in her eyes and she couldn't keep them from spilling down her cheeks. So, the Koreans thought of her as a cold, beautiful mountain, forbidding and lonely.

"Hey, I'm sorry." Roarke's voice was soft and pleading. "I was angry and I didn't mean to spoil your pretty nickname. But come on, Clover, don't make me feel like a bastard. Smile." He gently took her chin in his hand and pulled her face toward him. More tears rolled down her cheeks as Roarke slowly and sweetly kissed each drop until she buried her head in his neck and cried. He held her close, moving his fingers up and down her spine as his strong muscular arm clasped her tightly.

"I'm sorry, too. You hit a nerve and it hurt," Clover

said, wiping her tears. "Well," she said finally when she had collected herself, "I think it's time for lunch. Where's Myune?"

"I think he's playing down near those rocks." Roarke gestured toward the beach and stood up, grasping Clover's hand and pulling her to her feet.

Holding hands, they strolled down to the water's edge, then looked up and down the beach for the little boy. "Is that him?" Clover asked worriedly, pointing at a small figure clinging to the treacherous cliff.

"Yup." Without another word Roarke started to sprint down the beach. "Myune, get back here!" he shouted to the boy. "That's dangerous!"

A startled Myune turned and waved, then lost his balance and tumbled into the water. Clover screamed and broke into a run toward him. Roarke was there before her and jumped into the surf, emerging with a kicking and laughing Myune, who had been unaware of the danger.

Clover ran up to them, but stopped when she heard Roarke scolding the boy, who was just about in tears. She knelt beside him and gently pushed back his hair. "Myune, you promised not to go where you couldn't see me. You scared us, sweetheart."

Roarke wiped his face with his shirt sleeve. "I lost a brother when I was young from drowning in a swimming pool. I guess I was a bit harsh, but I know what water can do. It doesn't take much." He bent down and picked up the boy and tossed him on his shoulders. Myune laughed, and together the three of them marched off. Clover smiled. Myune, she realized, needed the company of a man. And so did she.

When they reached their blanket and picnic basket Clover spread a tablecloth on the sand and set out the lacquered bowls and plates, bamboo chopsticks, and spoons.

Mr. Yun had packed a gourmet Korean lunch and Roarke had placed a small brazier and a can of Sterno inside the basket to cook *bulgogi*—thin strips of marinated beef—a favorite Korean barbecue food.

Roarke lit the Sterno as Clover laid the beef strips on a platter. The fragrance of sesame oil and seeds, soy sauce, onions, garlic, ginger, and sake wafted from the meat.

"Mr. Yun does a delicious *bulgogi,*" she said.

"Smells good." Roarke smiled back. "What's in the blue bowl? I thought I shouldn't ask Yun."

"It's good you didn't. He's famous for it. *Oi seon.* Stuffed cucumbers. And not too hot, either."

Clover uncovered another bowl, revealing spring *kimchi*—a pickled cabbage that, next to rice, was *the* staple in Korea. More covered lacquered bowls held rice, *kochi chang*—fermented bean paste, and a rice-paper package full of toasted seaweed. Dessert was chestnut sweets—chestnuts mashed and mixed with honey, cinnamon, sugar, and brandy, and molded into flat round cakes one inch in diameter—and dried persimmons stuffed with walnuts, apricots, and prunes glued together with a sugary mixture.

"Can we have sweets first?" Myune asked, knowing Clover would say no.

"Dessert is for after the main meal, Myune."

"I knew you'd say no."

"Then why ask?" she teased.

"Maybe Roarke will let me."

"Not on your life, pal. The meal first," Roarke said, reaching for the *bulgogi* and dropping it on the hot, rounded grill, where it sizzled quickly. Clover picked the barbecued meat off the grill and placed it on top of the rice. She put a stuffed cucumber, a small amount of *kimchi,* bean paste, and seaweed on a plate and gave it to Myune with his chopsticks.

The morning ride and the excitement from his climb

on the rocks had given Myune a ravenous appetite. He stuffed the food into his mouth until his cheeks were full.

"I thought you always brought your manners with you?" Clover frowned at the boy. "Just because we're on the beach is no reason to poke food into your mouth like that."

Myune couldn't answer with his mouth so full, and instead shot Roarke a plaintive look.

"Just try not to choke." Roarke smiled.

"Will Sam eat this stuff?" Clover asked.

"Everything but the *kimchi* and bean paste."

Clover fixed a dish for the dog, who wolfed it down in three gulps.

"Watch your manners, Sam, or Clover'll get you," Roarke joked.

Myune laughed.

They ate their lunch in silence. Hunger and mild exhaustion, mixed with the torpid weather—muggy and overcast—made for three quiet people.

Clover watched Roarke, whose occasional glance back disconcerted her. She knew she was starting to like the man. She drew a quick breath. My God, she thought, he's handsome.

"That was good." Roarke pushed his plate across the tablecloth. "I like Korean food."

"Mr. Yun is a gourmet chef in that little shop of his. He does American food equally well," Clover said.

"So now what?" he asked.

"What do you mean?"

Another smile told her he knew he had a disquieting effect on her and she realized she was embarrassed again.

"Why aren't you married, Roarke?"

Roarke took a deep breath. "I don't like being tied down. I was raised in Boston, and after eighteen years of parties, stuffy socials, stuffier women, I revolted and left for college in California. Dad and Mom were extremely upset that I didn't carry on the family tradition and go to Harvard or MIT, but life in Boston was more than I could take. Everything there is tradition, like here, and I'm sick of it. I want to shape the future, not molder in the past."

"How are we to understand the future? I think the past is very important," she said.

"I know you do, and we'll be at loggerheads over that more than a few times in the next couple of years." He turned and frowned at her. He was serious, and the potential conflict appeared to bother him.

"Well, we can try to be civil to each other even when we disagree."

"It isn't being civil I'm worried about."

"What, then?"

"Us."

"Us? Is there an 'us'?"

He rolled over on his side and looked at her. "I want there to be. I'm attracted to you."

"Thank you. Coming from Roarke Devereaux I consider that a great compliment."

Roarke snorted and rolled on his back.

"Can I go play now?" Myune asked.

"Only if you stay on this beach. No climbing the rocks and falling in the water."

"Can I go up to the dig? I'll stay out of the way, I promise."

"Yes, you may, and please just watch, they're very busy, Myune," Clover answered.

Myune climbed up the hill toward the dig; Clover watched him until he reached the top and waved back to her.

"You nag that kid too much," Roarke said, still lying on his back, eyes closed.

"I'm responsible for him . . . and you saw what an adventurous soul he is. Besides, that's my business."

Roarke turned on his side and said, "Don't we agree on anything?"

"Looks like we don't."

He reached out for her, pulled her to him, and kissed the palm of her hand gently. She pulled away.

"Afraid?" he asked.

"Yes," she answered quietly.

"Of love or of getting hurt?"

"Both."

He placed his hand around her neck and pulled her down again. Before Clover could protest or pull away, his arms had completely surrounded her, his insistent lips exploring her neck and ears until she was at a point where then and there she had to tell him to stay away from her—or give in.

In seconds her mind clicked over the alternatives, but her body, long starved for a man's caresses, followed its own bidding, and she found herself responding to him. His hands, large and strong, kept her pinned to him, and she could feel his body ache for hers. How long, she wondered, had it been since he had loved a woman? Yesterday, or . . .

His heated kisses, his probing tongue, and gentle but firm hands moving from her back down to her soft thighs and then up to her breasts, made no secret of his desire to take her at that moment on the beach. She felt helpless to stop him and even more helpless to stop herself. She ran her fingers through his hair and then across his chest, feeling the warmth and hardness of him.

She opened her eyes momentarily. His eyes were closed, so she studied him as he kissed her. His tan skin, slightly roughened with an afternoon stubble, excited her. His black lashes, long and thick, his forehead with barely perceptible lines across it, and the two frown lines between his brows made him seem far more human than his pictures had. She felt a flush rise in her when he pulled away and gave her a wide grin, one of friendship and warmth. She smiled back. She liked him in spite of his gruffness and pig-headed attitude toward cultural history.

His finger brushed her nose. "Pretty," he said softly. "You're damned desirable, too. How could you possibly have escaped from all the single men here? I don't understand."

"None have moved me. I wanted to . . . to . . ."

"Love again?"

"Yes."

Roarke pushed her down on the mat. She was hypnotized by the gentleness of his light and sweet kiss and she felt uncontrollable warmth and delight rise in her.

He was so expert at seduction that only her inner feelings penetrated her mind and she hardly noticed that his hands were moving from her breast to her thighs. Only when she finally felt his caress becoming a prelude to lovemaking did she fully realize what he was doing.

She quickly pushed him away, and was surprised that he made no attempt to stop her. Then subconsciously she picked up the sound of Myune's laughter far away and it jarred her back to the realization they were on a public beach with dozens of workers and a small boy just seconds away.

"Roarke, stop please. Not here."

"In Cheju Dō next weekend?" He started to nuzzle her again.

"I don't know. You've confused me. I wasn't prepared for this."

"I'll bet," he said, and abruptly sat up. "You're so damned scared that you'll give something away, you're petrified."

"If you think that, why do you want me? Surely there's an easier mark somewhere else."

"I want you. And that's the sweet hell of it, love."

"Why, for God's sake?"

"You wouldn't understand." He rolled over on his side and looked out over the sea.

"Clover! Clover! Come quick. Come, hurry!" Myune called from the top of the hill.

Flustered, Clover brushed herself off, buttoned her blouse, and got up.

"Coming?" she asked.

"No. Not interested."

"It might be a find at the dig."

"I told you, I'm not interested in the past. You go and give me time to recover from your passion."

"Bastard," Clover muttered under her breath, glad to be away from him.

"Young Ni," he countered, and turned to her, smiling. "I'll change your nickname someday."

"I doubt it," she called back, laughing as she ran up the hill.

A granite block had been moved from the entrance to the tomb, but as happens so often in archaeology, the grave was empty. Grave-robbers hundreds, maybe thousands, of years ago had already plundered it. Not a single artifact or body remained. Extreme disappointment registered on the faces of the students, who silently turned away and began to clean up the site. The block was replaced and marked. Jin-Soo sat quietly on a rock to watch the slow and deliberate activity.

"Why isn't there anything there?" Myune asked.

"Someone has already found it and taken the things away," Clover answered.

"Where are the things?"

"I don't know," she said. "It happened too long ago."

"Oh." Myune looked as sad as the students, and was quiet for a change.

"Come on, Myune. We can't help here now. Let's go."

"You kiss Roarke?" he asked abruptly as they walked toward the beach.

Clover drew in a breath. Had he seen them earlier? "Why do you ask?"

"He like you."

"Roarke and I must get to know each other better before we kiss," she said, watching Myune fall silent again to think this over.

3

Clover walked slowly toward the rehab site, rolls of plans tucked under her arm. She felt annoyed. At Roarke? He hadn't talked to her since their picnic three days ago. And the planning activity was still hers, although she was reluctant now to suggest anything out of the ordinary for fear of Roarke's disapproval. Would the advisory committee, made up of older Korean men, turn away from her advice and defer naturally to the commanding Roarke Devereaux? It was hard enough to work as an equal in this country, but now she had to redouble her efforts to prove her worth, and Roarke could make life hell for her if he wished.

It was time to confront him professionally and come to terms with their differences. Rounding a corner, she saw that the wooden buildings to be torn down loomed in the morning mist and looked as if a sudden gust of wind would tumble them into a dusty, splintered heap.

Roarke stood on the crumbling gray-brick sidewalk just

ahead, his tall frame slightly stooped to catch the quiet voice of Prince Yee. The sight of Yee impeccably garbed in blue jeans and tee shirt startled her. And Roarke had gotten to him before she had the opportunity of introducing them. It was a small oversight that nevertheless put her at a disadvantage with the tradition-bound committee. Panic rose in her throat at the sight of Roarke's familiarity with the prince.

"Good morning, gentlemen."

Roarke smiled at her, his self-confidence maddening; or was it bold, undisguised arrogance?

Clover, determined not to let her sudden tremor of insecurity show, gave a slight bow to the prince, her eyes lighting up with amusement on the green alligator on his shirt; but she shuttered her expression to avoid seeming disrespectful.

"Good morning, Clover." The prince smiled. "Roarke and I have been discussing the destruction of these buildings. He has a very good suggestion."

I'll bet he has, Clover thought sourly.

Roarke gave Clover a wide grin behind the prince's back.

Prince Yee, unaware of the tension rapidly growing between Clover and Roarke, stood back from the site. "We'll tear all of the buildings down on the perimeter first. That will be done by hand. Then we will erect a sturdy chain-link fence around the site so our people can watch the wrecking equipment work on the rest of the buildings without danger of their being hit by falling objects." He turned to Clover. "You know the natural curiosity of my people. Without the fence they will get too close to the machinery, to see better. We don't want tragedy to strike our new neighborhood."

Clover nodded in agreement. It was a good plan. Score one for Roarke.

A flurry of movement behind them interrupted the

prince's description of Roarke's scheme. Five members of the advisory committee had arrived by the kamikaze-trained Seoul Taxi Company. A screech of wheels and a puff of smoke from the tires signaled to the passengers that it was safe to let go of the handholds and get out. Before Clover could step forward to introduce Roarke to the newly arrived men, one of them, Mr. Shin, held his hand out and greeted Roarke as an old friend.

"Roarke Devereaux, good to see you!" Shin said. "Let me introduce you to our committee members." Shin turned to the assembled men and said, "Gentlemen, this is Roarke Devereaux. He just completed the dam on the Soyang tributary near Chunchon. A marvel of engineering. Roarke was here as a major in the army corps of engineers when the main dam on the Soyang was started. We're lucky to have him on this project. Good man."

Roarke grinned. "Gentlemen," he said softly, and extended his hand.

"This is General Han," Shin said. "And Mr. Pak and Mr. Park, our bankers, and the Reverend Cho, a representative of the river-dwellers."

Apparently they all knew Roarke either personally or by reputation. Well, he did say he had been in Korea longer than she had.

As if she were no longer there or even involved in the project, the men chatted amiably among themselves. Korea outwardly accepted women in business, but by nature, or custom, or plain orneriness, women were still treated as nonpersons.

Only Prince Yee remembered his manners and turned to Clover. He said aloud, "Clover has the plans for the site. Why don't we sit over there and look at them?"

They all walked over to a doorstoop of a building and sat down on the steps. "We'll have to set aside a place later for work at the site, a small trailer, perhaps," Roarke said.

"That is a good idea." Mr. Shin said, beaming at Roarke.

Brilliant, Clover thought sourly. Roarke, she suspected, would try to hold sway over her committee. Only this wasn't her committee—it was the mayor's. And, she realized, this was no longer her project.

Clover spread a large map of the site out on the porch, turning it so it was aligned in the proper direction.

After a moment, Roarke asked, "What's that large green area, Clover?" He pointed at the map.

"It's a park. Green always denotes open space."

"I understand. But why put all of your open space in one plot? Let's spread it out. That way these apartments," his finger—a slender, brown, demanding finger—swept over the rows of apartments, shown in red, "won't be so crowded."

"I like that idea," Mr. Shin said.

The initiative had to be taken now or she would lose her influence forever with these men.

"Roarke, I think you had better study the plans for the apartments before you leap into proposed changes. Within each complex, we've designed courtyards, patios, and play areas. This is the communal park. If it is made any smaller, it won't serve its purpose."

Prince Yee now seemed to sense the potential rivalry between Clover and Roarke. "Clover is correct. The architects were careful about overcrowding when they designed the dwellings. Perhaps, Roarke, you would like to study the full set of blueprints in Clover's office. They are much too bulky for her to have carried them over today."

Roarke leaned over the plan, frowning. "Yes, I think I had better study them. I'm concerned about it."

Anger knotted Clover's stomach. She would be damned if she'd let him change a thing on those plans. That was not his job. She hastily returned to her commentary.

"The three churches and a Buddhist temple are scattered here." She pointed to four ultramarine shapes on the map. Before Roarke could interject again, she took possession of the discussion and held on to it. She quickly pointed out the placement of each major aspect of the new community as if it were a foregone conclusion that Roarke could not change. The men listened without comment. Her subconscious mind took in each member as her voice and knowledge continued nonstop to review what they had already decided on at their meetings.

She needed now, more than at the beginning, to be taken seriously. Roarke's presence was a greater danger to her career than the natural reluctance to accept her the men on the committee had shown even though Prince Yee had introduced her.

Roarke was a man with whom these older men felt more comfortable. A man whom the others apparently knew, whose charm, and masculine good looks could both destroy her carefully built rapport with the committee and the emotional wall inside of her that she had hidden all these years.

"And so, gentlemen, there it is. A year of your hard work and decisions in full color. Looks good, doesn't it?" Clover finished.

They all murmured and nodded. Even General Han altered his expressionless face to show approval.

Roarke still frowned. What the devil, she wondered, is bothering him now? She silently challenged him to try and change the plans. He would quickly discover that she wasn't easily bullied.

"I'll walk back to the office with you to look at the plans." His voice was demanding and arrogant and discordant.

Clover rolled up the plan as the men began to stand one by one. As if on cue, a familiar screech of brakes broke the tension. The same cab that had disgorged the five men earlier gobbled them up in a hail of good-byes. Prince Yee bobbed a bow to Clover and Roarke, got into a sleek Jaguar parked nearby, and roared off.

Clover stood stiffly, watching the urbane prince drive away. Shaken by her own fury, until now held in check, she turned on Roarke.

"You conceited S.O.B.," she blurted out.

"Dear Miss Clover, such language from a lady." He laughed.

Their eyes met: hers deep-green pools of unbridled rage; his darkly arrogant, amused, and infuriating in their bold self-assurance. He knew very well what he had done today and he knew she had taken complete victory from him.

"Well done, Clover," he conceded.

"You're nothing but a swell-headed bastard! Us friends? Not in a thousand years."

Roarke grabbed her wrist and twisted her around to face him. "I take a dim view of being called a bastard. My mother wouldn't like it, either." His eyes danced, a flickering fire suggesting ire and mock amusement.

"The shoe fits, old boy. And it *is* old boy, isn't it! Shin knew you."

"No crime in knowing people," he retorted, and let her go.

"Not as long as it isn't used . . . wrongly."

"Clover, I won that contract fairly. Just because you lost, don't try to explain it away by accusing me of dishonesty. Don't be a bad sport."

She walked away at a brisk pace. Did he win the contract fairly? Until now, it had never occurred to her that he hadn't. Besides, she told herself, she had not accused him of anything. Those were his words. It seemed to her that Roarke was a little too defensive—and that made her suspicious.

"Now, shall we review those plans?" Roarke had caught up with her.

Clover didn't answer. She would make him follow her. Let him come to her office. She would tell him what he wanted to know but he'd have to ask her on her terms.

She didn't look back once on the way to her office, but she knew that the sight of a tall American woman striding down the street followed by a tall American man had turned curious heads.

"I hope that nice little walk we've just had cooled your temper," Roarke said, collapsing in a chair as Clover sat at her desk.

"You must know how difficult it is for a woman to work here, and you're deliberately making it harder for me. What's the point, Roarke? Ego?"

"Look, you're brimming with resentment over my getting the contract. Tough. I did get it and that's that. Now get off that hobbyhorse of yours and try to be reasonable. Whether you or I like it or not, we have to work together."

"Then stop trying to undermine me. I won't stand quietly by if you do."

"I'm not trying to undermine you. If you're referring to my meeting with Prince Yee, it was by accident. I went out to the site early and he was there. It would have been rude to ignore him just to wait for you to make formal introductions."

Clover glared at him.

"Look, let me give you a piece of advice. You want to be equal but you're acting like a spoiled little girl who didn't get her way. Learn to accept defeat with the same alacrity as success. Even we superior men have our ups and downs. But we're such good fellows, we take it in stride. Be like a man, be a good sport, and you just might be equal someday." Roarke grinned at her.

Clover melted. Even though his words were deliberately provoking, she knew he was right. She had been acting spoiled and immature. She would have to stop reading sinister motives into everything he did. She smiled back.

"Good," Roarke said. "Now tell me about the committee members. I know Shin, but the others are a blank to me. What are they like to work with; and the committee, is it just a placebo or does it have a real function?"

"The committee is a real working committee. Apparently everyone on it has a direct line to the mayor and city council. General Han is the power but Prince Yee is the most respected one, and even Han will bow to the prince's suggestions when they conflict with his own. General Han? Now, what can I say about a man who has never spoken directly to me since we've met? I don't understand him, except that he is a true old-fashioned Korean and it's obvious he doesn't like to have me here," Clover said.

"He made quite a reputation for himself in Vietnam. I was there for about six months building pontoon bridges with the corps. Han was in command for five years. Touchy as hell and ruthless as Genghis Khan."

"He's in arms manufacturing now. I wondered about his place on the committee, but city hall wanted a diverse group and they got it."

Roarke smiled. "Park and Pak. What're they like?"

"I call them the Bobbsey Twins. If one wants something, the other does too. Bankers."

"Ah, that's where I've heard of them."

"They're taller than the others but mentally Han and Shin dwarf them. They go along with any scheme as long as they see it making money for their banks."

"And Cho. He seems more modern than the rest."

"Uh-huh. He's a good man. A bit of an advocate for his people, but that's expected. He's afraid that because the river-dwellers are poor the others will disregard their needs. He keeps the committee honest, so to speak."

"I like Yee," Roarke said. "Seems like the perennial intellectual."

"Don't let that smooth exterior fool you. He's a gentleman through and through, but he will get his own way in the end. A planner's planner."

"Good for you." Roarke laughed.

"I find that the Koreans are modern in their thinking, but, ironically, when they began selling their services to foreign countries, they temporarily lost some of their more innovative workers. Now they have to import expertise to make up for it. Planning is new to them and there is a reluctance to accept long-range schemes, especially if it means drastic change. You know how people hate change, and Yong Dong Pō has been the way it is now for hundreds of years. People are scared, and I don't blame them." Clover cocked her head at Roarke.

He was making notes on his yellow pad. Without looking up, he said, "And you, Clover? What about you?"

"What about me?"

"I want to know what makes you tick," he said.

"I'm a trained planner. I got my master's in planning from Berkeley four years ago and joined Thompson Associates after John died. When I became an associate, I bid on this job, got it, and moved here."

"Where did you learn to speak Korean so well?"

"During my undergraduate years, I was an exchange intern with the State Department. They assigned me to the embassy in Seoul. I picked up the language then, and when I knew I was coming back I took a crash course to polish my speech."

"Uh," Roarke said. "The real Clover McBain will remain hidden for a while." His voice was quiet and she liked to hear it. What was it about his voice that intrigued her so?

"Do you mind if I see those plans now?"

"Not at all. Park yourself at the worktable and I'll bring them to you."

For the remainder of the morning, Roarke bent over the plans for the new neighborhood, making notes and grunting. Clover tried to work, but his disturbing presence made her uneasy.

She watched him as he pored over the plans. His thick, black hair and hard, muscular neck were particularly masculine. When he turned his head to write on the yellow pad, Clover could see the long lashes hovering over his eyes. His mouth was sensuous, the kind women want to kiss just to see what it would be like. And his hands—Clover watched them, too. He had hands to match the rest of him. Handsome, demanding, arrogant, and so damned sensuous that Clover thought it unfair that so much animal sexuality should be concentrated in one person.

He finally turned and caught her staring at him. She blushed and tried to look away, but his eyes riveted on hers and she was mesmerized.

"Lunch?" he asked quietly.

"Yes. I was thinking about how hungry I am. Where do you suggest?"

"My place?"

"Not at all. Somewhere near here."

"Someplace safe, I take it?" he growled good-naturedly.

"Yes. Mr. Yun packs a pretty good basket and we could eat down at the river."

"Seaweed and sea urchins, squid, and *kimchi.*" Roarke laughed. "Not my idea of a quiet lunch with a beautiful woman."

"Roarke." Clover was exasperated with him. He turned toward her, sitting on the high stool at her drafting table. His body was bent slightly as he leaned on the table, studying her. His face was a maddening aura of overconfidence, his straight, almost lantern jaw jutting out, causing her to see him in the same appraising manner that he had looked at her on their first meeting.

She liked his looks, his voice entranced her, and his hands gave her the feeling that if he did caress her it would be the most incredible sensation she ever had. Too bad they had to work together; that precluded any familiarity between them beyond a professional relationship.

"And?" he asked.

"And what? What do you want me to say? For God's sake, Roarke, we have to work together, and I know I sound like a broken record, but let's keep our relationship on that basis."

"Do you think you can? You fairly melted in my arms Saturday. No resistance. No doubts."

"You egotist. Why did you have to come here and bedevil me? Leave me alone, Roarke. I don't want involvement and I don't want a repeat of our beach scene. Why can't you just let it go at that?"

"I can't and I won't," he said, again his voice of that quiet, forceful, authoritative tone. "Why not involvement? What's eating you?"

"Just because a woman does not want you, there's something eating her? My dear Roarke, you are not the answer to my prayers. I know that must come as a shock to you. But that's the way it is."

A deep laugh bubbled up in Roarke and he stood up, held his hand out, and said, "Come on, Clover S. McBain. Let's have a peaceful lunch on Mr. Yun's seaweed down by the river."

She hesitated, then got up from her desk. Together they walked down the back stairs rather than trust to the elevator and get stuck, God forbid, between floors.

Mr. Yun packed ham-and-swiss-on-rye sandwiches, two cold cans of Coca-Cola, and tostito chips. Clover smiled at Roarke, and they took the basket and walked to the river.

"Mr. Yun's shop is a continuous surprise. When I was

in there Saturday, I swear I didn't see that deli in the back."

Clover laughed. "Mr. Yun didn't have that deli until I arrived. When I wrinkled my nose at the squid, he and his wife began stocking American foods. The Korean office-workers saw me walking off with ham and swiss and complained to Yun that they would like some too. Next thing, the deli."

"Already you're changing Yong Dong Pō. Who would have thought ham and swiss in YDP!"

They sat quietly along the river bank on the rocks that jutted out near the bridge.

"The river is rising. Look at the marker," Roarke said, pointing toward the metal measuring stick at the edge of the river.

"At least, thanks to you engineers, the dam is finished and the Han won't flood as much. But I'm still anxious to get our river-dwellers on high ground. How long do you think it'll take to prepare the site for building?"

"I'm afraid about five months. Did you know that underground stream that runs along the outer edge of the swale is a potential hazard?"

"No. Will that pose much of a problem?"

"Depends. If you would change your plans to allow for it to surface, we could even have it running through the grounds as a decorative touch and make it a floodplain. Could save us problems years down the pike."

"How much change?" Clover was growing wary.

"Quite a lot, but I'm not being arbitrary, Clover. It might cause some of the apartments to be undermined in a fifty-year storm."

Clover was quiet. She had vowed not to let him change those plans and now she might have to compromise after all.

"I'll think about it. Let's draw up some alternatives and present them to the committee. It might have to go to the mayor for final approval. That would be another delay. He spends a lot of time thinking about changes and often delays projects unnecessarily. I like the man but I prefer not to present more for him to look at than is absolutely necessary."

"I know what you mean. I've had the same problem with the governor up at Chunchon."

Clover stretched out in the spring sun. A hand reached over and pulled the two large pins out of her hair to let it fall around her shoulders.

"You should wear your hair down. It's beautiful," Roarke said.

Clover refused to acknowledge his gesture. How could she convince him to stop making overtures to her? She had held herself back from romance and involvement for four years now, until Roarke Devereaux came along. What right had he to assume she would fall willingly into his arms and his bed?

She was determined to fight him. She wouldn't let him pull her down into the abyss that she had spent the last four years crawling up from.

She felt his eyes on her back and once again the need to let go of her past agonies washed over her like the brown waters of the Han River washed over the rocks nearby. Roarke would leave a mark on her if she let herself succumb to his earthy sexual charms.

"You're too beautiful and desirable to let yourself grieve forever over a dead husband. Four years is a long time. Don't you think it's time to let go?"

"No. It wasn't just John that died that day."

"You?"

"Part of me. When John and I married he didn't want children because he said it would be the one thing to stop him from racing. When he was ready to stop, then we'd have a baby. I got pregnant, Roarke, and I was afraid to tell him. If I had, he might not have gone out on the track that day. So you see, I really was responsible for John's death. The terrible irony was that I miscarried two days after the crash. I killed my baby, too. I can't forgive myself or forget. So please understand, I don't want to play emotional games with you."

"Hey. Stop punishing yourself. Okay, I'll leave you alone. I can't compete with some giant guilt complex that makes you dead set on ruining your life. You're more interested in feeling sorry for yourself than you are in me or any other man in the world, aren't you?"

Roarke's harsh words were spoken with quiet authority, and she resisted every syllable. She was angry at him for probing at her inner feelings far beyond the point to which she had invited him. He had penetrated the depths of her self-hate and now he analyzed her as if she were a specimen in a jar. And it hurt. She didn't like those feelings blatantly dissected. It had become more comfortable for her to keep them buried deep within her.

"Back off, Roarke," she ordered tersely. "You don't know what you're talking about."

"I hit it pretty accurately and you know it. Maybe someone had to."

"Let's eat and go back. I don't like it when our discussions turn to hurtful things."

"You mean to things that smack of unwanted truths," he said grimly, opening the wrapper on the sandwich and popping the top on the can of Coca-Cola. Clover rifled through the tostitos, munching loudly to drown out her thoughts.

They ate in silence and it seemed to Clover that the only time she and Roarke got along was when they were quiet.

They walked back to her office. After Roarke finished looking at the blueprints, he said a curt good-bye and left. Clover's office took on a dark loneliness it never had before. Roarke had brought with him a warm companionship that Clover didn't value until it was withdrawn.

She studied the silk wallpaper, swirling with fantastic birds and flowers in muted stone-greens and silvers. The hanging scrolls in bright colors, the rosewood monk's chairs with blue and white cushions, and the pots and vases, expensive antiques she had collected from China, Hong Kong, and Taiwan, all looked as if the spirits that had been living in them departed with Roarke. Carefully decorated to blend in several Oriental cultures, the room seemed suddenly harsh.

She heard Sam bark and a voice quiet her. Her heart reached out, wanting to get up and see what the commotion was. Instead she waited, momentarily unsure. Sam barked again. This time Clover used the noise as an excuse, to herself, to find out what Roarke was doing.

There was nothing in the hall that looked out of place, so she walked to his office. She cautiously opened the door and looked in. He had not yet found a secretary, so Betty was helping him settle in.

"He's in there," Betty said, smiling and pointing toward the door.

"I heard the dog bark and thought something was wrong."

"Of course. But he's still in there." Betty's maddening appraisal of the situation irritated Clover. She walked through the door to Roarke's office to be greeted by a chaos that boggled the mind. Papers, boxes, books, and sacks of dog and cat food littered the entire room.

"Hi, come in," Roarke called cheerfully. "Not the elegance of your office, but it sure as hell is more friendly."

Clover's eyes took in the sight. On top of a huge pile of cardboard boxes a scroungy yellow, one-eyed cat perched just out of reach of Sam.

"That's CC. I found him wandering the streets of Chunchon. I knew sooner or later someone would make a stew out of him, so I picked him up and brought him home. CC, meet Clover . . ." Roarke stopped and said. "What's your middle name, so I can introduce you properly?"

"Scheherazade," Clover said.

"What?"

"Don't bother with the jokes. I've heard them all."

"Where on earth did you get that name?"

"My mother is an incurable romantic and Clover was the heroine in one of those romance novels. Scheherazade you know, of course."

"Personal friends." He grinned back.

"I thought she would be, knowing you."

"But you don't know me, Scheherazade," he quipped.

"I can pretty well guess from what I've heard."

"Have it your way, Young Ni!"

Clover reached up and touched CC. "Hello, kitty."

"I have a real collection of orphans at home. Come to dinner tonight. I promise no advances, touches, or probing questions. You'll be safe. I have a viper for a housekeeper and she'll be there to protect your reputation."

Clover liked the feeling she had when Roarke was around. He had taken the warmth from her office, the spirits that lived in her vases and pots, and brought them into his chaotic world. The thought of spending a few hours with him tonight, even in his home made her feel good. All of her mighty resolutions began to melt away and she decided to spend the evening with him. Her strict rules would have to be altered slightly to accommodate a new sensation beginning to grow in her. Something indefinable but . . . there.

"Fine. Where do you live?"

Roarke's eyebrows shot up and he looked genuinely surprised.

"You did mean it? The invitation, that is," she asked.

"Yes. I just expected a long, dragged-out argument. I live on the other side of Nam Sam Hill. Que Do She

Street. The blue-and-yellow house with the pink wall around it. Sounds like bad taste in colors, but it works well. I have a cherry tree that has just begun to bloom and it spills up and over the wall so you can't miss it. Want me to pick you up?"

"No, thank you. I'll drive. Can I park in front?"

"No problem. Everyone parks with the right side of the car on the sidewalk to leave room for other cars to pass."

"What time?" She was reaching up to scratch CC's ears, trying to act casual.

"Seven okay?"

She turned and smiled. "Seven is fine," she answered, a little surprised at the surge of lighthearted joy that raced through her, a joy that persisted all through the remainder of the day.

Just before quitting time, Betty walked in with papers for her to sign. "What're you wearing tonight?" she asked.

"What would you suggest? It's apparent that you and Roarke have talked this over."

"That flowered sheath you got from Hong Kong."

"A little formal, a little too exposed. I don't want to suggest anything."

"You wore it that evening Doctor Lee took you to the university dinner. And I know you weren't trying to be sexy. It's just that everything you put on makes you attractive that way."

"I'll wear a gunnysack."

"Funny. But seriously, I like Roarke and he's a real nice man. Give him a chance. Please, Clover. You're so lovely. You have so much to give."

"Betty, I know you mean well. But I'll repeat—I have to work with the man. Getting romantically involved will make it too difficult. If he thinks getting me in the sack will help him usurp my authority, then he can forget it. I won't compromise my work."

"I wasn't suggesting you 'get in the sack' with him."

Betty turned away indignant. "But if I were your age, you'd have competition," she said closing the door.

Clover grumped as she reached for the papers to sign. One was the letter to David Thompson telling him that they did not get the Phase II contract. On an impulse, Clover dashed off a handwritten note at the bottom of the letter expressing serious concerns over the awarding of the contract. The nagging suspicions that had been plaguing her about Roarke had to be passed on to David. It was her responsibility as a principal of the firm to tell him how she felt. But, at the same time, Clover felt a pang of guilt. Was it her own acute disappointment that indeed "tried to explain" her failure away, as Roarke had said?

Betty peeked through the door, grinning. "It's time to go home. 'Night, CSM," she said, and closed the door.

4

The residential area behind Nam Sam, the hill in the middle of Seoul, was one of the few pieces of real estate not totally destroyed by the North Koreans when they overran the capital during the war. Some of the houses were Japanese-built and had subsequently been modified into Korean houses. Tile roofs hovered over high walls that surrounded every home. The walls were predominantly pink brick, the roofs red or blue tile, and the streets a dull gray brick used universally as street material in Korea.

The winding main street up the hill was narrow and finding a particular house was maddening because each house was numbered according to when it was built rather than its location. One had to have precise directions to a friend's house or spend hours looking for it.

Clover had taken more time getting ready for her dinner with Roarke than she had planned to; so she was late. Her hair was swept up with two lacquer combs inlaid with mother-of-pearl holding it in place, and she wore a modest blue silk flowing dress by André Kim, Korea's hottest designer. The dress left everything to the imagination, but was still high-couture enough to be chic, even in European circles.

Roarke's house was situated on top of the hill overlooking Seoul. His magnificent cherry tree, whose branches fell over his courtyard wall in a pink riot, was visible from blocks away. She found a space for her car, parked it, and got out. She could smell *bulgogi* cooking on someone's grill and her stomach growled in anticipation.

Walking toward Roarke's heavy wooden gate, she was amused to find an Irish coat of arms on it. She knocked and waited, expecting to see Roarke's smiling face as he threw the gate open.

Instead a wizened old lady, dressed in a traditional high-waisted Korean dress opened the gate just wide enough for Clover to see two small black eyes and a wrinkled face. She looked Clover up and down appraisingly, then reluctantly opened the gate to allow Clover to squeeze through.

The woman called in Korean to Roarke, who appeared with two drinks in his hands, smiling his wide smile.

"Come in, if Gee will let you," he said, and pointed to two chairs and a small table in the middle of the courtyard.

The courtyard was an Oriental paradise, landscaped with flowering cherry, azalea, and forsythia; a sparkling *koy* pond; and an abundance of fruit trees bursting with blossoms. The L-shaped house sat serenely facing the garden, with walls made of movable wooden panels, lacy in their carved beauty. Teak columns separated the panels and were carved with philosophical homilies from Korean Buddhism. Potted palms in Korean blue-and-white pottery jars graced the porch; here and there small birds and animals watched her from partially hidden vantage points.

Her eyes must have reflected her surprise and admiration.

"Like it? More to your taste than my office, I guess."

"It's . . . beautiful, Roarke. You live in a Garden of Eden complete with tame animals. What are they?"

"My menagerie. That's a *Gachi* bird. Its wing was broken and CC was about to make a meal of it when I rescued it. It's been around ever since thumbing its beak at the cat. I pick up stray and hurt animals and nurse them back to health. I always had a veterinary hospital in my backyard when I was a kid. Actually I'm pretty good at it."

She knelt at the edge of the *koy* pond. Plashy waterfalls spilled over rocks, and the large carp sparkling in bold oranges, whites, reds, and blacks crowded around her, anticipating a handout. Roarke reached into a box nailed on a post nearby and tossed a handful of feed to the voracious fish.

"Drink?" He handed her a glass. "V.O. and Seven?"

"Yes, thank you. How did you get this house? I thought I was lucky just to get a modern apartment."

"Just happened along at the right time. An elderly couple was moving to an apartment and wanted to sell it. So here I am." He handed the drink to her as Mrs. Gee, his housekeeper, came out with sizzling beef on sticks with a hot, sweet-and-sour dip. She laid the hors d'oeuvres on the table, gave Clover a warning look, and disappeared.

"Thank you," Clover said to the retreating back. "I don't think she likes me."

"Mrs. Gee? She doesn't like anybody. Quite an old crone but very good at keeping my disordered life straight. I actually think she resents any female intruding on her domain. I've had her for years—brought her with me from Chunchon."

"Mother substitute." Clover laughed.

"Hardly. I can't picture Mrs. Gee mothering anybody."

"Thank you for having me tonight. I was looking forward to this," Clover said gently.

"Really? I would have thought you'd have brought a bodyguard with you."

"Let's not start in on each other tonight, please?"

"Absolutely. Bite me tongue, lass." His Irish accent made Clover laugh, and she relaxed.

But Roarke's offhand remark about getting the contract fairly made her doubt that she could trust him completely. It nagged at her, and she felt she had to find out just how he did get that contract. At least then she would know the facts and could deal with her emotions more reasonably.

"Tell me about yourself, Roarke." She wanted to try and fathom this man whose life was always a subject of gossip, her knowledge of him based on that gossip.

"I was born in Boston. I lived in Boston, and if I had stayed there I would have died of boredom in Boston. The end."

Although Roarke had tried to make the statement humorous, it was tinged with cynicism. "Care to tell me why the bitterness?" She sipped her drink and kept her eyes on Roarke. He was looking into his drink, plumbing the depths of his fierce dislike of his hometown.

"Do I sound bitter? Don't mean to."

"You sound like there's more to your life than three short sentences."

"All right. You told me your most intimate secrets, so I'll tell you mine." He paused, took a breath as if the telling of it required extreme fortitude. "My father is Jacques Devereaux, a rich—very rich—banker, and my mother is Annie O'Roarke from a lower-middle-class family in South Boston. If you know anything about Southy, it's the pits. A working-class, dogmatic, cliquish part of Irish Boston."

"How on earth did your mother and father meet?"

"My mother fought her way out of Southy with education and determination. She is very beautiful. They met at a cocktail party. But she was still from Southy, and society had inherent difficulty accepting her. They did, finally. But who could be impressed with a social stratum with such ridiculous standards?"

"And she felt the snub," Clover said quietly.

"Not exactly. Her origins in Southy are a long story."

"Tell me. I'm fascinated." Clover tucked her feet under her and settled back for what promised to be a good story.

"My great-great-great grandfather was a sea captain whose ship sailed from London to the Middle East. His daughter had a love affair with someone the family disapproved of, so they packed her off on his ship to cool down.

"When he returned two years later, he brought with him a baby girl born to his daughter. The daughter had died in childbirth and the baby was deposited with his long-suffering wife. Anyway, the baby girl was very dark—black hair, black eyes. Gossip labeled her part Arab.

"Great-great-great grandfather never said so, though, and he went away. His ship went down in a storm a month later and the baby was left without much ancestry and a lot of speculation as to its parentage. It seems our family has one child every generation who turns up black-Irish—dark hair, dark eyes, and so forth. Like me. Like my mother. Annie O'Roarke Devereaux is the most beautiful woman in Boston, like a Gypsy princess, all sparkles and light, and Dad's 'a fine figure of a man,' as the Irish would say. Quite a couple. He's tall, French, born in Boston, too. One look at my mother and he was in love. They married and had five children. All of us kids had the best schooling, including dancing lessons. Can you picture me in white gloves at Madame Groysa's dancing classes?"

Clover couldn't imagine it and laughed.

"So I'm the one child in this generation who turned out dark. My brothers and sisters were brown-haired, green- or blue-eyed, and I was the black sheep. I wasn't the most cooperative kid in town, and soon acquired a reputation for it. Mom and Dad worried about me. When I decided to go to school in California, they probably thought a change of scene might help my attitude. Then I chose to work in Korea and they gave up. They think I live in a barracks and carry an M-1 around. You know how people still think of Korea."

"I still don't understand," Clover said.

"My real problems came when I discovered that how a person is treated generally by society depends on how much money he has and who his ancestors were. I began to hate the trappings of the rich because I saw my mother's relatives a lot and they treated me like a snooty rich kid from Beacon Hill and Dad's relatives, on the other hand, treated me like a poor kid from Southy. I got tired of it. I like money, don't get me wrong. But to me noblesse oblige is as valid today as ever, and money isn't the criterion I judge people with. Money is a means to an end only!" Roarke set his glass on the table with a thud.

Clover nodded. But she knew she had not heard the whole story. His life did not sound entirely as if he had anything to be bitter about. She wanted to probe, but decided against it.

"What happened to your brother, the one you said drowned?"

Roarke's eyes clouded over. "It was in the swimming pool at a friend's house. I think Mark hit his head when he dove off the board. Anyway, we thought he was teasing us when he didn't come up. By the time we realized he wasn't fooling around, and we got him up to the surface, it was too late. Actually only a minute or two passed, but that's all it takes. He was my favorite."

"I'm so sorry, Roarke."

"Yeah, so am I." Roarke looked away, still grieving for the long-ago-lost brother. "He was only ten years old. I was seven. And it happened so fast. He was supposed to be watching me, since I was the one who always got into trouble. And I was the one to pull him to the surface. I'll never forget what death looks like."

Neither Clover nor Roarke spoke for a long time. Clover knew the anguish Roarke felt and shared his grief with her own hard-won understanding. Guilt. Did they both suffer from that malady?

As the sun went down a slight chill crossed Clover's arms and she rubbed them.

"Let's go in. Mrs. Gee is probably finished preparing the dinner. I didn't dare ask her what we're having, so we'll tough it out together."

Roarke did not have to fear dinner from Mrs. Gee. *Bulgogi* grilled lightly over a small charcoal fire at the table, with mild spring kimchi served in small side bowls, along with pine nut soup, and a fiery pepper sauce that stood nearby, untouched by either Clover or Roarke. There was a light salad, crisp Korean pears, and an almost sugarless dessert that tempered the spicy meal. Clover liked most Korean foods and so ate the meal with enthusiasm, washing it down with hot tea. In all she was more relaxed than she thought she could be.

Then Roarke shattered the fragile atmosphere. "You're an enigma."

"How so?"

"Well, your names, for one. Scheherazade. She was a fiery, lustful, giving woman; and Young Ni is a cold mountain. What does Clover stand for?"

"A normal, upper-middle-class woman from a bland, peaceful community south of San Francisco. I had a non-eventful upbringing without much trauma and about as normal as one can expect in this turbulent world."

"Boring?"

"I didn't think so until I met John McBain. He opened a new world of glamour, excitement, and danger to me. Without using my head one little bit, I married him. The only exciting thing I'd done before that was my year in Seoul. And actually that went smoothly, without any real excitement or danger. I made one trip to Hong Kong and loved it, and that's about all."

"Been to Hong Kong this tour?"

"No. I've been so busy I haven't had time. My furniture and clothes are all mail-order, except for what I buy here. I'd love to go again. This time I have enough money to buy what I want."

"I'm going in about two or three months for equipment. Why don't you take off and come along?"

Clover looked at Roarke suspiciously, her eyes narrowed.

Roarke laughed. "I couldn't lure you with Cheju Dō so maybe Hong Kong."

"Maybe." Clover was surprised at her answer.

"Who'll go with me—Young Ni or Scheherezade?"

"Neither. Clover. And if you don't stop leering at me, Roarke Devereaux, Clover won't go either."

Roarke's sudden touch as he reached over for her hand sent electric shocks through her body. She pulled away.

"Don't," he said quietly. He got up and walked around to her side of the table. "Walk in the garden with me. Here's something to ward off the chill."

"Thank you," she replied as he gave her one of his bulky sweaters.

They strolled around the small garden, *tiki* torches burning the fragrances and beauty into her brain. She felt tipsy from the pre-dinner drink. Roarke put his arm around her and stopped. He pulled her to him as the heady fragrance of fruit blossoms rested on the warm, humid night air.

As on the beach, her body refused to listen to reason and she felt a hot flush of desire rush to her head, making her dizzy and incautious. It wasn't until Roarke's sensuous mouth plundered hers that she gave up entirely trying to fight this man who forced his way into her well-ordered and safe life. Her lips parted and she felt his warm, moist tongue dart into her mouth; her senses reeled, her mind overpowered by his body and hers. Her hands caressed the back of his neck and her fingers ran free through his hair. At that moment Clover would have succumbed to Roarke if he had not suddenly pushed her away.

"I can't compete with two ghosts." The bluntness of his statement was like ice cold water splashed in her face. All of her reason and common sense came flooding back and she tried to pull away, ready to do battle.

"Roarke, that was damned unfair."

"I didn't mean to bait you. I find you desirable. And more. You're spirited, and I told you I like that. All my life I've been trying to find a woman I could love and live with, and believe me I've tried quite a few. But they were so darned concerned with 'getting me' that they melted and gave in without a fight."

Clover stifled a laugh.

"Oh, hell, I'm saying it wrong. Let me try again. Clover, I like a woman who has a mind of her own and one who'll give me a run for my money."

Clover laughed out loud this time.

"Oh, forget it. I can see by the look on your face that I'm not getting through." He turned serious suddenly. "Try and not be too suspicious of me. Maybe you'll see me as I really am. I have a wall around me, too. Maybe not as impenetrable as yours, but it's there. I want a woman to break through that wall, because I'm sure not going to open the gate for her."

Clover looked up at him, comprehending and not comprehending. She saw Roarke one minute as a vulnerable man who deserved to find an understanding woman and the next minute as arrogant and overbearing.

She turned away and walked toward the house. Roarke hesitated, then followed her, his face a mixture of hurt and anger.

"I thought we weren't going to do this," she reproached quietly.

"So did I, and I had no intention of kissing you. But your mouth was there, inviting me in spite of the fact you said you didn't want it."

"You misunderstand. It wasn't what you did, it was what you said."

He groaned helplessly. "You mean Young Ni versus Scheherazade? I hope in the end Clover is the woman I find."

She drew in her breath sharply. What did he mean by that? From what she knew of him, Scheherazade would be just his style.

"After-dinner drinks and then good night," he said.

He handed her a small cordial glass full of a sweet, almond-flavored Korean liqueur, and they stood by a *tiki* torch. The fire flickered over his face, shadowing the harsh dark planes and outlining the full, sensuous curve of his lips. He didn't move toward her but his desire was clear in the tension of his muscular frame.

"Good night, Roarke," she whispered, and the sound of her voice in the night, soft as if they were in an intimate embrace, made her reel with dizziness. He caught her arm.

"Do you need a ride home?" he asked.

"Just the opposite. I need to get away from you." She turned toward the gate, walking as fast as she could, thinking only of escaping. She was startled when Mrs. Gee stepped out from the shadows to open the gate.

In a soft Korean voice she said, "You come back," and let Clover out the gate. The significance of the inscrutable Mrs. Gee inviting her back was lost in the emotions of the moment.

What the hell is happening to me? Clover wondered. She jumped into her little car and careened down the hill as far from danger as she could get.

Her lips tingled from Roarke's kiss and she caught a whiff of his spicy after-shave lotion. In her altered state of anxiety, she had failed to notice she was still wearing his sweater. Shaken, she pulled the car over to the curb and trembled. She wrapped her arms tight across her breasts and hugged the warm wool of the sweater close—as close as she would have hugged Roarke had he been inside it.

"Oh, God," she cried aloud, "it's happening all over again."

5

How was your date with Roarke?" Betty Witherspoon poked her head in the door and greeted Clover. "Oh," she said, crestfallen when she saw the look on Clover's face.

"We have to make changes in the plan," Clover lamented. "And the evening was a disaster. I shouldn't have gone. I knew better."

"Want to talk?" Betty asked.

"No. Just don't encourage him, please." Clover managed a weak, irresolute smile at Betty, who frowned.

"He's so nice, Clover," Betty said. "I understand you have to maintain a professional atmosphere. But . . ."

"But what? Good morning, ladies," Roarke said, pecking Betty on the cheek as he edged past her and through the door.

"Good morning, Roarke," Betty answered. "I'll go get the morning mail, Clover," Betty said, and diplomatically disappeared.

Roarke plunked rolls of plans on the worktable and

turned to Clover. She watched him as he placed his hands on his hips as if to challenge her—his eyes dancing. "I made all the necessary changes that we can work with—together."

Clover rose slowly and walked over to him. She was all too aware of his maddening scent, the hard muscles of his arms, and the sensuous tilt of his prideful chin.

"May I look at them?" she asked as politely as she could under the trying circumstances.

"Be my guest," he said, gesturing to the rolls. "Look, Clover, let's scotch the tension. I didn't make the changes arbitrarily. We can stick to the original idea almost totally. And about Friday night . . ."

"I don't want to talk about Friday night. I shouldn't have come. But the dinner was delicious and you were nice to invite me. I guess I acted a little rude by leaving so abruptly. But, I told you, I don't want a relationship with anyone. I lost my head and I'm sorry."

"I got hell from Mrs. Gee after. She likes you, Clover."

Clover looked up at him, surprised. "Really? I wonder why?"

"Do you always question why people like you?" Roarke asked.

Clover stopped. She always questioned people's motives, but no one had ever asked her why. She shrugged, and unrolled the plans to look at them.

For a moment Clover was struck speechless, so impressed was she by Roarke's sensitivity toward the original plan. His execution of the engineering design for the swale was beautiful. He had enhanced the project by bringing the underground stream to the surface, creating a picturesque park complete with duck pond and waterfalls.

"It's beautiful. I really like it, Roarke."

"Good. I worked all weekend on it. And I thought about you while I did. I wanted to please you, Clover."

"Thank you," she said, not knowing what else she

could say without dredging up all the feelings that frightened her away from him Friday night.

He put his hand on her shoulder and his fingers, caressing and warm, found their way to the back of her neck.

Clover pulled away. "Please, Roarke. Don't."

"Why not, damn it? For God's sake, we like each other, so why force ourselves to reject our feelings? It's stupid, Clover."

"Because I'm not sure of my own feelings. Of course, I'm attracted to you. Who wouldn't be? Even Betty told me if she was my age, I'd have competition. But does that mean a love affair? Can't we just like each other and leave it at that?"

"I don't know," Roarke said. "If we were in the middle of a war zone and the only two Americans for miles around, I would question our attraction. But we aren't in a war zone and there are plenty of attractive men and women for each of us. So why can't we treat it as you and me, love? Would you push me away if we were in New York or San Francisco, or is it just Korea?"

"How do I know? It *is* Korea, not New York or San Francisco. I really don't know how I would react to you Stateside."

"Probably the same. Little scared Clover. Afraid of a man's affection. Once bit, twice shy. Right?" Roarke demanded.

"Let's change the subject. We don't seem to communicate very well on that level."

Roarke sighed, exasperated. He leaned over the worktable and pointed out significant changes in the plans and how they would have to be accomplished to keep the project on schedule.

"We have to give this to the advisory committee. I'll call them later today and see when they can all be here. Tomorrow, if possible?" Clover asked.

"Sure. Fine." Roarke answered. He looked at Clover

and smiled. "If they go to the mayor, though, we'll have to wait at least a month for a decision."

"I know. But we can't make major changes like this without consulting him. Know anyone at City Hall?"

"No one who counts." He laughed.

"Okay. I'll call Prince Yee and ask him what he wants to do. These drawings are so good we won't have to have them done over. You really do beautiful work. Do you remember asking me if you suit me?"

"I sure do," Roarke answered.

"Well, you certainly do, if this is a sample of your work. I'm really pleasantly surprised."

"Thank you so much," he answered, and rolled the plans up. "I'll guard them with my life."

"Did I offend you?" she asked.

"It's just that you have such stereotyped ideas about engineers. I'm not a clod. I can draw and I can plan. It's all part of the four years I spent at CIT. Give me credit for a little intelligence and sensitivity!" Roarke picked up the plans and smiled. "I said enough. Let me know when the committee will meet."

"All right, Roarke," she said.

"In the meantime, you might try thinking about this, too." He tilted her chin and kissed her, once firmly, twice lightly.

Roarke left and Clover sank into her chair behind her desk. She knew he was right. They weren't in a war zone, where relationships are based on mutual fear and loneliness between two very frightened people clinging to each other. This was modern-day Korea—rich, exotic, and cosmopolitan. So why was she fighting her intense desire to possess Roarke? Why was she so reluctant to begin an affair with him? Was it fear of rejection?

Or was it the sure knowledge that if she did have an affair with him she would fall in love. Was it the uncertainty of love that was really stopping her? Love. Could she ever love again with the same intensity she had had with

John McBain? And was Roarke the man? Would Roarke be the kind of reckless, possessive man who would tear her heart from her chest and without another thought use it and toss it aside? She didn't know.

As the next few days went by she found herself trying to push her stray thoughts of him aside when they surfaced, unable to decide exactly how she wanted to deal with them. But she could not keep her ambivalent feelings toward him from invading her innermost musings.

The committee and the mayor of Seoul worked with unheard-of speed in accepting the changes to the plan for Yong Dong Pō. Clover and Roarke had worked hard to make the changes palatable to the committee members, who in turn had bombarded the mayor and his aides with demands for a quick decision to get the project going. Clover stood in awe of action that usually would have taken months to accomplish. Within a short two weeks, the mayor said yes to the changes.

Roarke and Clover celebrated with a lunch from Mr. Yun's deli. As they relaxed by the Han River, Roarke said, "Here's to Prince Yee. I've never seen anyone work so fast before. Especially here in Korea. Shall we toast the mayor, too?" Roarke laughed as he held his can of Coke above his head.

"To Prince Yee and the mayor," she called back. "And to getting the project started."

"We'll begin site preparation Tuesday," he said.

"Why Tuesday?"

"Because on Friday afternoon, Saturday, Sunday, and Monday, we'll be in Cheju Dō pheasant-hunting."

"Oh? How nice. Who's going with you?"

"Just you and me, doll," Roarke retorted.

Clover pretended to look around her for another person. "Me?" she asked. "Did I say I was going to Cheju Dō?"

"Not yet. But you will," Roarke answered.

"Look, Roarke. The last two weeks have been very pleasant. We've worked damned hard on the project without an uncivil word to each other. I've enjoyed it, actually. Let's not spoil all that by trying to dredge up a personal relationship."

"I think you're being childish. I'm asking you to go with me for a few days of relaxation. When we begin site preparation, we'll both be so exhausted from work we won't be able to move at the end of the day. We need some time off. Seven days a week is too much, even for me. I need to let go. Ever been to Cheju Dō?"

"No . . . but . . ."

"It's one of the most beautiful places in Korea. I've remodeled a thatched-roof cottage on the beach. All the comforts of home with the quaint feeling of old Korea. You'll like it. I have reservations on Korean Airlines for Friday, late morning. The tickets are paid for!" Roarke squinted at Clover as if he wasn't sure if she would throw something at him or accept.

Clover thought about it. She could keep her thoughts of Roarke at bay during the day, but at night—that was entirely different. Something about the humid sweetness of night blossoms and the soft touch of night air against her moist skin made her wonder what might have happened in his garden if she had not gone home. If it had happened now, would her decision have been the same?

Her lips curved as he looked at her quizzically—not expectantly. He wasn't that sure of her feelings, and she was perversely glad.

Suddenly Clover said, "All right. I'll go. It's against my better judgment, but I'll go."

Roarke looked up at her, his eyebrows raised in mock surprise, but he smiled. "Good. Let's drink to that, too."

Clover felt excited about the trip, and Friday was only a day away. Whether or not the feeling would last, she found it exhilarating to enter the world of the truly living again. Roarke had given her that much, and she was accepting it.

Cheju Dō Island was indeed the most beautiful place Clover had seen; and Roarke's cottage was enchanting. She felt as if she had been transported into a magical world of sun, sand, the thundering East China Sea, and the mystical Cheju Dō rock that thrust like a mountain skyward to disappear in a single, puff-white cloud at its peak. From outside the cottage that perched several hundred yards from the surf on a golden-sand beach bid her welcome, its rice-thatched roof whispering conspiracies to her in the warm breeze coming from the water. Inside, Clover could not tell she was in a cottage. It was decorated with bamboo, rice-paper walls, and lacquer furniture. The kitchen and bathrooms were modern; the rest of the rooms were in posh Oriental style that was comfortable, but exotic enough for the imagination to run rampant across history. For someone who denied any feeling for the past, Roarke had given his "cottage" the look of a wealthy, eighteenth-century Korean nobleman's house.

Clover realized the new setting underscored the new feelings inside of her. She had suddenly, or maybe not all that suddenly after all, changed. She was no longer afraid of Roarke or of the consequences of loving him. She had decided, quite deliberately, that she was prepared to love him. And, in fact, that she would encourage him. She couldn't explain to herself or to anyone the sudden metamorphosis; it was there and she welcomed it.

"Ready?" Roarke picked up two rolled *tatami* mats and several towels as he spoke.

"Let's go," she answered cheerfully.

They ran to the beach, laughing and joking about nothing. Roarke was wearing bathing trunks and Clover ran a little behind him so she could admire his body—

tanned, sleek as a panther, and muscular. After he dropped the towels and mats on the sand he plunged into the water and yelled to her that it was cold.

Clover tested the water with her toe.

"Cold? It's freezing!" she yelled back.

"It'll knock the socks off of you at first, but it's like the Scandinavians jumping from a sauna to the snow. Very refreshing. Come on, try it!"

Clover stepped in and waded up to her knees, when a wave hit her full-front and knocked her down.

"Roarke, help!" She cried jokingly, "I'm numb!"

She felt warmth filter through her as Roarke's arms scooped her up. He stood her on her feet.

"Let's swim and then get out. Too much of a good thing, and all that."

Clover followed Roarke out beyond the waves and swam vigorously. But the cold began to slow her and she turned to swim back to the beach.

"I think you've had enough swimming today," he said laughing as he effortlessly matched her stroke.

They laid out on the mats to let the sun warm them. She stopped shivering as Roarke laid next to her, touching her body with his, setting her on fire with his intimate caresses.

"I'm getting warm now. Thank you," she said.

"I know. I can feel it."

He kept his hand on her back, his fingers caressing her gently, kneading her sore muscles—muscles weak and tired from her swim. Instead of soothing her, his body set hers afire.

Roarke leaned over to her. "It's different with you," he whispered. His fingers brushed across her back lightly; his dark, erotic eyes riveted on her profile.

"What's different?" She felt a wild impulse to cover her face as Roarke's stare unnerved her. She wanted to react but didn't know how.

"Being with you, talking to you, just you," he answered. His hooded eyes moved seductively over her neck and shoulders to her barely concealed breasts, held precariously behind her scant bikini. She held her breath, deeply aware that Roarke's eyes had languorously wandered to a soft pink nipple showing itself brazenly. If she dared breathe, it would fall out completely.

She finally stared back at him, refusing to give ground. Roarke's eyes were his weapon—caressing her most intimate places—and she was helpless to stop him or her own runaway hunger. Her nerves were taut with wanting him.

She looked away, then shot another glance at him. His face was taunting and veiled, his eyes suddenly downcast, with thick black lashes hovering over his shadowed cheeks.

Then he looked up, catching her frank expression, and smiled, his eyes revealing a blatant sexuality. He knew she wanted him and he knew he would have her.

He was reading her mind. She knew he would play his cat-and-mouse game with her, but she didn't care.

The strong scent of sea air clung to the humid afternoon, cloying and thick. Bursts of wind swept in from the south, turning the whitecaps into thundering waves that crashed onto the sandy beach.

Clover reached for her robe, but Roarke's hand caught her wrist and pushed the robe away. With no effort, he pulled her down next to him and held her close. She offered no resistance as his now insistent lips grazed her forehead and burned a trail over her nose, chin, throat, and down to the shameless nipple. The bikini bra strained against her breast until he deftly unhooked it and plunged his mouth over her smooth white breast.

Clover groaned and her hips moved imperceptibly against him. He gently bit her shoulder as his hand began a long, slow movement up her leg—teasing its way to her warm thighs.

She held still on the now darkening beach, savoring

every movement of Roarke's lips and hands as they explored her.

Clouds scudded almost violently across the azure-green sky, blotting out the white hot sun. The breeze blew steadily and their *tatami* mats flapped around them.

"A storm," he mumbled from between her breasts, "one of those 'come-quick' ones . . . any minute." His mouth and tongue seared her skin, pressing against her flat, soft stomach.

"Roarke . . . I . . ." Her voice was raspy; words flowed in fitful syllables. "Roarke . . ."

"I know Scheherezade, I know . . ."

A gentle rain began to fall as the breeze surrendered to a hard wind. The humidity soared as the rain increased.

"I'm going to make love to you, Clover S. McBain," he murmured, "but not here. I want you without the rain and wind. Just us. Now." He wasn't asking her, he was quietly stating a fact, and she accepted it silently. He stood up and looked down at her imperiously, smiling. He held his hand out and as she struggled with her bikini bra, she reached for his outstretched hand and found herself pulled up easily against him.

His rain-splattered face betrayed him as a messenger of Neptune: seductive, mysterious, dangerously sexual. He lowered his head to her; his lips burned her mouth as his strong, demanding hands cupped her buttocks and held her tightly against him—his pulsing body exuding scorching desire.

Roarke slowly released her and she felt her knees buckle. He grabbed her arm. "Steady, sexy lady." He laughed. He scooped up the mats and led her to the cottage. Inside, he dropped the mats, shut the door with his foot, and guided her toward the bedroom.

Without ceremony or words, Roarke looked into her eyes as his fingers quickly unhooked her bra and reached for the bikini bottoms.

Locked onto each other's eyes still, Clover felt the warmth surge in her as Roarke untied her bikini bottoms and let them drop. She fumbled with the string holding his bathing trunks up.

"Need help?" he whispered, a wide grin on his face.

She felt the heat rise to her face.

"What a time to blush." He smiled even wider, his white teeth flashing in the dim light.

But his smile disappeared when he stepped out of his bathing trunks and his hand encircled her waist, pushing her to the mattress on the floor. He pressed her against him, his mouth and hands again burning trails of desire over her skin, awakening the eager hunger she had felt on the beach.

A hot, tingling sensation coursed through her, and she shuddered as it spread rapidly from her throat to her eager breasts, and then to her thighs, consuming her with a craving for Roarke's body. She wanted to possess him as he planned to possess her.

Her shaking fingers reached for his hair and slid down his neck to his back, feeling his muscles ripple under her touch. Her whole body shivered as the storm increased with thunder, lightning, and rain, providing appropriate orchestration for her rampant emotions. Reason, common sense, and any comprehensible thought had vanished, leaving a white heat only Roarke could quench.

"Roarke . . . love me . . . please, love me," she rasped over the raging storm outside.

He pulled her closer, pressed her to him until she screamed for him to give her the sweet, promised love she needed.

His knees pushed her legs apart and Clover could feel him straining against her. But he teased her, driving her to a wild pitch of sexual need until she begged and pleaded with him to give her release.

His mouth savagely silenced her, his tongue plunged in

to probe and claim every inch of her. He bore down on her with unbearable ecstasy, tormenting her, promising a wildness of love she was frantic to have.

After the long, agonizing kiss, Roarke's body twisted against her, his hand seeking her most intimate places, hot and moist from his excruciating caresses. Still he explored her with hands and tongue.

Then without warning he suddenly plunged into the searing heat, unleashing a fury that made the storm outside seem like a quiet spring rain.

Clover felt the hard promise of Roarke's thrust—deep and demanding. Her body burst into fire, burning, unrelenting, matching his hard male thrust with her own counterthrust, raging until a final piercing cry signaled total collapse for both of them.

Neither spoke nor moved. A heavy breathing against each other's sated body was drowned out by the rain. Roarke moved slightly, allowing Clover to breathe easier. He held her next to him as though he was unable to caress or kiss her; as though his mind and body were in a state of semiconsciousness.

She watched his face for a long time. He held on to her possessively until his lashes fluttered closed and he was asleep, so deeply asleep that the hard lines of his cheeks softened and his mouth curved upward in a smile.

As if an unspoken word flashed between them, Roarke and Clover woke together. How long had they slept? The storm still vented its fury on the cottage. The day had darkened until only flickering shadows crossed their faces, revealing and hiding the emotions awakened in them.

"Okay?" he whispered.

"Yes. You?"

"Weak but still living." He laughed softly.

Clover tucked her head into his neck, kissing and biting his ear.

"Keep that up and I'll seduce you again."

"*You'll* seduce *me?*"

"Somebody'll get seduced. It's all the same in the end. No?"

Clover wriggled closer to Roarke and pulled a sheet over them. The night was strangely hot and humid, but the combination of rain and humidity made the cottage warm one minute and cool the next. She shivered.

He held her tight as they lay still, listening to the storm: crashing thunder, brilliant flashes of lightning, the sea beating against the shore, trees bending and whipping, and branches falling on the thatched roof—normal sounds of a summer storm.

His hands moved from her shoulder, down her arms, and over to her breasts. At his touch her nipples became hard and eager again. His fingers gently kneaded her breasts and as his hands dropped to her stomach; his tongue encircled her impatient nipple.

She explored him as he explored her. Her hands moved across his chest, the hair there damp and matted. She felt herself go weak as she moved lower, shyness coupled with an intense curiosity to hold him, explore, and learn as much about his body as he had about hers.

He encouraged her to use her hands to excite him. "Arouse me, Clover. Touch me. Don't be afraid of me."

She reached down and was erotically moved to touch him, feeling his pulsating desire for her. She caressed him until she could stand it no more and pulled him to her, demanding of him all he could give.

It was her need, her satisfaction, that must be fulfilled. She moved her hips lovingly against him, insisting, demanding; the sweet gentle, voracious rhythm of love rippled through her.

"My love, my Clover, what are you doing to me?" he cooed in her ear. His teeth nipped at her neck; his quick, desperate kisses rained down on her face as his passion increased to fever pitch. They cried out together in painful, needful ecstasy, and suddenly lay still while their loving release echoed around them.

She had taken all she could from him and he was utterly spent. He pulled away and lay on his side, keeping her close to him. His face showed surrender to her.

Holding her tight, his voice was throaty. "You're quite a woman, Clover. A man could spend his life in bed with you and never miss the rest of the world."

"Um," she replied.

"What does that mean?"

"Hmmm. I'm too tired to answer. You're not the only one who feels slightly drained."

"The conquerer is tired?" he asked.

"She is." Clover's laugh sparkled, and she looked at him. "Roarke, I wanted you, even that day you came into my office and put your foot on my desk. I fought the feeling, but . . . but I can't fight it anymore. I guess I'm brazen or something. But I . . . I . . . wanted you." She really wanted to say 'I love you' but was afraid to shatter their fragile alliance.

He laid his head on her breasts and she cradled it lovingly. She felt satisfied, her need fulfilled, her conquest of this man complete. Let the storm blow, let her doubts splinter her thoughts; it didn't matter. She had her life in her arms. She had her promise of tomorrow.

The next day, buoyed by her new feelings of confidence and love and experiencing a touch of possessiveness, Clover accompanied Roarke to the local country club to join an organized pheasant-hunt. The confusion there was compounded by milling dogs and the pleasant chatter of Koreans who had gathered around the head guide for instructions that no one listened to. The sun was shining and the vestiges of the previous night's storm had vanished. In all, it promised to be a beautiful day.

Several local Koreans waved to Roarke, greeting him with polite familiarity. He chatted amiably with them until a tall, imposing, heavy-set Korean approached. He introduced himself as a Mr. Hwang. He carried a pigeon-grade Browning over-and-under shotgun and two sleek golden Labradors followed him adoringly. A wealthy man, Clover noted quickly. He frowned at Clover, the only woman who had come along, and politely but coldly accepted her as though she were a necessary evil.

Roarke leaned over to her conspiratorily. "Have you ever fired a shotgun before?"

"Ummm," she answered noncommitally as Mr. Hwang motioned for them to follow him. They walked toward the outfitter's shop and entered. Roarke showed the outfitter his two shotguns. They were serviceable but had not the beauties of Mr. Hwang's Browning.

Roarke bought licenses and two boxes of shells for himself and Clover.

"I'll show you how to load," Roarke said as they left the office with Mr. Hwang walking behind.

Clover smiled and thought about the many weekends she had spent happily tramping and shooting with her father and uncles as they hunted on Kings Mountain around Woodside, California, where she was raised. Roarke, and Mr. Hwang, too, would have a surprise in store when the shooting began.

The large, noisy party began the short trek to the elephant train that would take them to the base of the mountain a few miles away, where they would break up into smaller groups, each with a guide, to hunt the delicacy that Koreans loved above all other food.

The rich Koreans used Cheju Dō as their playground, emulating American and European mores, eating exotic, imported food. Today millionaire industrialists, high government officials, bankers, and others whose money burned holes in their pockets marched up to the train for the day's sport. Even the dogs wagged their tails, anticipating the fun ahead.

Mr. Hwang shared a seat with Roarke in the train and

eyed Clover suspiciously. "You shoot, young lady?" he asked.

"Some," she said, not wanting to lie outright about her abilities.

"Stay with me; I'll help you. A lady should not be alone on a hunt."

Clover smiled at Roarke's expression. He couldn't say "no" to a man who was making an obvious gesture of friendship. But the set of Roarke's jaw told her that he would stick very close to both her and her instructor.

"Thank you. Have you hunted here before?" she asked Mr. Hwang.

"Every weekend during the season," he answered.

In Korea it is considered impolite to ask someone what he does for a living. But Clover knew the type. He was an industrialist, she decided, and let it go at that.

The train stopped at a flat plain in the foothills of the mountain. Clover, Roarke, and Mr. Hwang, along with the guide and the two dogs, got out and began a slow march out onto the plain through the weeds and bramble.

After a short walk, the dogs stopped and pointed. Clover stepped forward and flushed first one pheasant, then another. She raised her shotgun and expertly downed them both. The dogs ran off in a frenzy of excitement, bringing back the succulent birds.

"For you, Mr. Hwang," Clover said, presenting the birds to the startled and flustered Korean.

"You shoot well, young lady," he said without emotion or expression.

The next few minutes were spent reloading, and trekking farther along the plain in the foothills.

Again the dogs stopped and pointed. Clover whispered, "They're yours, Mr. Hwang."

Mr. Hwang stepped forward and flushed the birds. He raised his gun toward the cock and hen and downed them. The dogs rushed forward and came back, depositing the birds at Mr. Hwang's feet. Mr. Hwang said, "Now I present a bird to you, Clover."

Clover smiled and said, "Thank you. This will make a delicious meal tonight, won't it, Roarke?"

Roarke, a sour expression on his face, whispered to her, "You're very good. Is there anything you don't do well?"

"You only asked me if I had shot before," she answered sweetly.

Roarke followed behind Clover and Mr. Hwang as the noon sun glared overhead. Again the dogs pointed, and Roarke stepped forward to flush the birds. Roarke aimed and downed a lone hen. As he fired, another bird farther away flew up and Roarke fired again, getting the second bird.

"Six birds! That's a good shoot," Clover said.

"I think we should celebrate at my house tonight," Mr. Hwang said. "I'll have my cook make a dinner fit for nobility. We'll have a *Kisang* party."

"Oh, I'd love that," Clover blurted out.

Mr. Hwang frowned and said gently, "A *Kisang* party is normally for men only."

"That's all right, Mr. Hwang. I've been to one. Although the Mama San almost dropped her teeth when I walked in, it worked out well."

Mr. Hwang had no choice but to include her. "Then you will not mind a few girls from the local *Kisang* house?"

"No. Of course not." Clover laughed to herself. A *Kisang* party was strictly a male affair, but she looked forward to seeing the ceremonies and eating what promised to be a very good meal.

The afternoon lunch was served and eaten hungrily; the rest of the day was spent hunting. In all they shot twenty large and plump birds, and Mr. Hwang sent the guide to his weekend house with them so the cook could get started on the dinner.

As they walked away from the country club after the hunt, Roarke said, "I don't look forward to dinner tonight."

"Why, for heaven's sake? Sounds like fun."

"Only when you've had an abundance of *Kung Jung* and don't care if some dolly is rubbing your leg under the table or not."

"Why, Roarke, I'm surprised you aren't an avid Kisang-goer."

"I am," he said. "But not when my date is along. I don't think your presence is appropriate."

"What was I supposed to do all evening while you were at the party? Did you think about that?" Clover was angry and hurt with Roarke's attitude.

Roarke, on the other hand, simply veiled his emotions and looked grim.

Mr. Hwang's weekend cottage resembled an old Korean temple. When Clover admired his porcelains, he explained that Koreans had revived the ancient celadon and the famous blue-and-white of the seventeenth century. These were reproductions that were now commanding high prices throughout the world. On close examination, only the perfections of the porcelain told her it was new and not the old, coveted celadon and the Yee Dynasty blue-and-white that she loved.

"Please, take this one. I can tell from your eyes that you like it," Mr. Hwang said, picking up a large vase of blue-and-white porcelain brushed with red.

"I can't take that. It's priceless," she said, backing away.

"Nonsense; it was fired three weeks ago. Hardly priceless. But in a couple hundred years, it will be," Mr. Hwang said proudly.

"Oh, Mr. Hwang, what a beautiful gesture. I feel so badly that you thought I wanted it."

"Take it," he said gruffly, and Clover knew that she must or risk insulting him in his own house.

"Thank you," she said taking the beautifully proportioned vase in her arms. During the rest of the house tour, she kept her eyes lowered and her mouth shut lest he give her more of the beauty she admired. Roarke smirked and she saw him watching her as she secretly cherished the artwork, most of which was new and exquisite.

"The cook tells me dinner is ready and Mrs. Kang's girls are waiting for us," Mr. Hwang said, laughing. Turning to Clover he asked, "Are you sure you won't eat alone? It isn't that we do not want you, I just don't want you to be uncomfortable."

"Only if my presence will make your guests uncomfortable, will I eat alone. But it won't bother me!" she said cheerfully.

The low, long, rosewood table was set with celadon ware filled with Korean hors d'oeuvres. Beautiful *Kisang* girls stood nearby in their summer *Kisang* dresses. Clover had never seen the summer uniform—a high-waisted skirt with thin straps barely covering their tiny, rosebud breasts. They bowed respectfully, but each one showed on her face obvious disapproval that one of the guests was a woman—in the latest André Kim designer dress, no less.

Mr. Hwang signaled his guests to seat themselves on the pillows. Clover sat next to Roarke as his "*Kisang* guest." The other men, mostly middle-aged, wealthy, and overweight, each had a *Kisang* girl to feed him, pour his *Kung Jung,* and chat amiably with him.

Since most of the male guests were on Cheju Dō without their families, it was anyone's guess what would happen after the party. Normally, the parties were held in Seoul, and the men went home to wives and kiddies afterward, worked up enough to give their long-suffering spouses a good run around the bedroom. But if a Korean man had no family obligations, he might well enjoy the ministrations of his *Kisang* girl through the night.

Clover oohed and aahed appropriately when the servants brought in Korean fancy fire pots in sterling silver and placed them on the table. Each *Kisang* girl reached out with chopsticks and began to pick out the mixture of beef, abalone, vegetable, and seeds marinated with sesame oil for her assigned guest. The sizzling fire pot sent streams of oil and steam skyward.

The noise and happy chatter drowned out Roarke's comment. "You're going to feed me, aren't you?" he asked Clover as she reached over to fill her own plate.

"The blazes I will. You want food, you have to reach for it yourself," Clover shot back good-naturedly.

"Some *Kisang* girl you turned out to be," he retorted, reaching for a Chinese mushroom and a tantalizing piece of hot and spicy beef.

After the fire pot, an array of *kimchi* arrived, extremely spicy and mouth-burning. Clover reached for a small portion and placed it on her plate. She nibbled at it and drank a sip of *Kung Jung,* the potent Korean rice wine.

"I propose a toast," Mr. Hwang said, holding aloft a water glass full of his own *Kung Jung.* Almost one hundred percent alcohol and served warm, a few glasses of the fiery liquid could incapacitate the most determined drinker.

Mr. Hwang went on, "To our American guests," and all of the male guests picked up their glasses and drank the wine down in one gulp. Roarke followed suit as Clover sipped at hers, smiling sweetly as the men laughed at her for being a coward.

After the *kimchi* and another toast, after the raw meat with pepper sauce, a jellyfish dish, assorted mixed vegetables, and yet more toasts, the pheasant came. Under a crystal dome, it was the highlight of the extensive meal. It deserved, and received, a toast, as did everyone at the table who had shot a bird that day. Clover was glad she had chosen a dress without a waistband: now she could eat some of everything presented without feeling pinched and sick.

The evening was more than pleasant; it was a raging success. Clover watched discreetly as the *Kisang* girls plied their ancient trade, keeping the men fed, happy, and drunk.

Not until a novice stands up does he or she feel the effect of so many glasses of *Kung Jung.* Most Koreans can temper their intake and stagger home with only a little help. But when Roarke stood up and turned to thank his host for the beautiful dinner and congenial atmosphere, a surprised look crossed his face, and he slowly crumpled to a heap on the pillows. Clover herself felt a little off balance after nursing one glass all evening, but Roarke, being a male guest, had had to drink an entire glass with every toast. Six or seven glasses had simply proved too much, he had quietly and elegantly passed out.

6

Clover steadied herself momentarily against a side table as a tipsy laugh stifled itself in her throat. She watched Mr. Hwang and three inebriated guests pick up Roarke and revive him.

Roarke was in no condition to drive home, so Clover snatched the car keys from his hand.

"I'll drive him home," she announced. "Come on, Roarke. Let's go."

Someone thrust the porcelain vase in her hands and she clung tightly to it while the men helped Roarke out to the car. Clover placed her vase in the back and tried to get into the driver's seat.

"I can drive, Clover." Roarke sounded surprisingly sober all of a sudden, but she knew he would be dangerous behind the wheel.

"No, Roarke," she said sternly, pushing him over to the passenger side. Mr. Hwang and his guests laughed uproariously. Roarke growled at her but did not appear to have the strength to argue.

Clover thanked Mr. Hwang for the party, started the car, and drove off. Although she was far more sober than Roarke, she had difficulty driving home through the unfamiliar and poorly lighted countryside.

When they reached the cottage, Roarke opened the car door, stumbled out, and weaved his way to the front entrance. "Thanks for the evening," he said angrily, and walked in.

Clover followed, feeling perplexed and angry herself. Why should Roarke turn on her? At least she had stayed by him through the ordeal. She just didn't understand this man.

Inside the cottage she stumbled over the edge of a rug looking for a safe place to put her precious vase. She swore softly at herself for not watching where she was going, put the vase down, and turned back toward the bedroom to look in on Roarke.

He had been the perfect *Kisang* guest, polite and cooperative, drinking when called on to do so, eating everything on his plate, and telling his share of stories in his impeccable Korean. Passing out was perfectly acceptable, if not necessarily macho. He had not lost face, but he would be ribbed about it in the future and have to suffer the teasing good-naturedly.

With indulgent amusement she studied his face. A peaceful smirk had been temporarily branded on it, but when he woke in the morning the expression would certainly have been exchanged for a remorseful glower. A *Kung Jung* hangover was ferocious! She threw a blanket over him and went into the guest room.

The ride home had completely sobered her and now she was wide awake. She sat on the edge of the bed in deep concentration. It had been an incredible two days. She and Roarke had made love at her encouragement—a risk she was more than willing to take. For the first time in years, the cold mountain had thawed. Roarke had scaled the fortress and she prayed it all would last—the euphoria, the feeling of sexual fulfillment, the need to be part of a man's life. But an insidious doubt had creeped into her mind. Roarke was too volatile and unpredictable. She knew deep inside nothing would last with him.

Slipping her dress off, Clover let it fall to the floor, and went into the bathroom. She turned the cold water on in the shower and let out a screech as it struck her warm skin. The lingering odor of cigarette smoke, incense, *Kung Jung,* and *kimchi* were washed down the drain in the fragrant lather. Later she shivered alone in bed, until deep sleep finally claimed her tired body and mind.

"Pull down the damned curtain!" Roarke roared as the morning sun struck his red eyes.

"Talk about a bear with a sore head," she murmured, dipping a cloth in cool water, wringing it out, and placing it gently on Roarke's forehead.

"Please, Clover, leave me alone. Don't even talk to me. Be very quiet and keep the room dark," Roarke moaned from the bed.

"Will you be up to going home tomorrow?" She ignored his plea for silence.

"Yeah. Just let me sleep." He rolled over cautiously and closed his eyes. "*Kung Jung* never affected me like this before," he groaned from the pillow. "I wonder what the hell was in it?"

"You drank seven full glasses. What did you expect?" she replied unsympathetically.

"Uhhh . . ." was the painful reply.

In spite of the hangover, his disposition had improved slightly, she thought. She pulled a sheet over him, patted him gently on his bare shoulder, and tiptoed from the room.

A sharp rap on the front door startled her. She opened it and saw Mr. Hwang's cook grinning at her, a lacquered covered bowl in his hands.

"For Mr. Dever-oh," the cook said, shoving the bowl at her. "Make head feel good, Miss Young Ni."

Clover was so surprised that a cook in Cheju Dō knew her Korean name that she didn't question him as he waved good-bye and hurried to Mr. Hwang's waiting car. The chauffeur waved and drove off with the cook.

"Thank you," she said weakly to the departing car.

"Roarke?" she called to the reclining figure burrowed deep into the bed covers.

"No," he protested.

"Mr. Hwang sent soup. Drink it," she ordered softly.

"No. Go away."

"Please, Roarke. I'm sure it's good for you and you need something in your stomach."

"No! I can't," he groaned. "I told you to leave me alone!"

Clover sighed and left Roarke. She tasted the soup and decided *she* needed it. With a relish that made her feel a little guilty, she drank the soup and then settled into a chair to read.

The next morning, Clover was up early and heard noises from Roarke's bedroom. Without thinking, she went in. Roarke was standing at his sink shaving, his naked body glistening from a recent shower. Stupefied, she stood in the door-way, watching him.

"Do you always stare at naked men?" he asked. The angry tone of the night before was back again.

"No. Sorry. I . . . uh . . . I thought you might need help.

"Thank you, but I've had enough of your help."

Clover walked over to him slowly. He reached for a towel and wiped the shaving lather from his freshly shaved face.

"May I ask what the hell is bothering you?" she asked calmly.

Roarke looked at her with an expression she had seen only once—when he was ready to fire one of his foremen. Now that visceral anger was turned toward her.

"Do you really need it spelled out, Clover?"

She fought to keep her temper and hurt under control. "Be so kind, since I've apparently missed something."

"Boy, have you ever," Roarke snapped. He walked over to an open suitcase on his bed and started tossing his clothes into it. "First you show me and Hwang up at the hunt by outshooting everyone."

"You're angry about that?" she asked incredulously.

Roarke continued as if she hadn't spoken. "You invite yourself to a male-only party, intrude on a male domain, and take charge like a spinster school marm after I get smashed. I've spent years building a rapport with these men. I plan to live and work in the Far East for a long time, and in one evening you tear down everything I've been trying to build, causing me to lose face and become a laughingstock."

"You hardly knew those men . . ."

"Korea's a small country. My . . . our . . . little scenario will be common knowledge before we even get back to Seoul. Thanks for taking over my life and embarrassing the hell out of me!"

"But—"

"But? My God, Clover, one night in my bed doesn't place a ring in my nose. Nothing's changed!"

Clover lost control and without another thought let Roarke have it with both barrels. "Wait a damned minute. Do you think you're the only American working here? Remember, Mr. Devereaux, that I, too, have to work with these people and I must do so on an equal basis, with the entire culture against me. As I recall, you tried to undermine me when you first arrived. Now you have the gall to accuse me of making you lose face? You're the one who couldn't hold your *Kung Jung*—not me. You passed out—not me. I had to drive you home if we were to make it in one piece. And as for my outshooting you! Well, tough! I just happen to be better at some things than you are. If that hurts your fragile ego, that's too damned bad!"

Clover was close to tears. She had said more than she should and said it more stridently than she intended. But it had welled up in her along with the hurt, the terrible anger, and the indignation.

The room was suddenly too quiet.

"At least we both know where we stand with each other. I never should have allowed you to seduce me that first day in your office and on the picnic at the tomb site." Roarke's face contorted into a grin as he turned away. It so infuriated her she screamed at him.

"Damn you. Why can't you take this seriously? You just insulted me, shouted at me, and now you're laughing!"

He sobered. "Believe me, I am taking it seriously. I just thought your histrionics were getting a little out of hand."

By this time her anger had subsided, and she shook her head. "I think we had better call off this vacation before one of us kills the other. I had hoped . . ." Her voice trailed off.

"Wipe that disappointed look from your beautiful face. You'll have many more opportunities to sample my wares! We can kiss and make up when you understand your place in this country."

Clover grabbed a towel and snapped him hard with it on his bare buttocks. She dropped the towel and ran from the room, shouting, "You're the most conceited, arrogant, maddening man I've ever met."

Roarke's laughter followed her to her room, where she packed her suitcase and dressed, angry that her own emotions could not be controlled. But she was disappointed. Disappointed that what she had hoped would be the beginning of a long relationship had turned out to be the bitter end of it. And disappointed, too, that he had succeeded in humiliating her and reading her thoughts—thoughts she wanted to keep private.

They rushed to the airport in cold silence and discovered that their plane had developed mechanical troubles, delaying their flight until afternoon. Clover tried to concentrate on a paperback novel to keep the surface calm from breaking into another argument. Roarke, on the other hand, made friendly conversation with her as if nothing had happened that morning to ruin a perfectly good vacation.

How could he sit there and pretend that once bitter words were spoken they could be forgotten so easily? She simmered, fighting the urge to answer him with more than polite grunts. It was at times like this, when Roarke changed his emotions like a chameleon changes color, forgetting how he had hurt her, that her suspicions took hold. She wondered if he was really that callous and so lacking in normal feelings that he could rage at her one minute and pretend the next that nothing happened. If he was like that, then a minor thing such as winning the contract because of knowing the "right" people wouldn't bother him at all. He could simply go on as if nothing untoward had taken place. Clover sank deep into her thoughts, wondering bitterly what she had let herself in for.

After they landed in Seoul, it was too late to go to the office, so they retrieved their luggage and drove to her apartment.

"Need some coffee?" she asked, knowing he would refuse.

"No, thanks. I'll see you at work tomorrow. When site preparations begin, I start work around six. I like to supervise it from the first shift to the last. We'll all be exhausted during the first couple of weeks. That's why I wanted this weekend to relax." He looked at her sheepishly and got out of the car. He carried her luggage to her apartment and left.

Clover looked around her. She didn't want to be alone in her own apartment now. Roarke had awakened something in her, then effectively destroyed it again, but she still wanted that big work-obsessed man and his ridiculous hangover to be sitting beside her on the sofa, even if his ego was getting the upper hand in their lives.

On the sofa? She laughed aloud, then stopped as she heard a sound of pain, not amusement, in her voice. In her bed, that's where she wanted him—not on the sofa.

The restless feelings she had dreaded were hitting her full force. She argued with herself. She was an adult. She didn't need someone who ran hot and cold, who was capable of tender love one minute and who then could turn on her the next, when she broke one of his stupid rules. Roarke wasn't capable of love—only a physical act that he loosely referred to as love.

There it was again. Love. Just what is love? What does it feel like? Was it the intensity of feelings she had had with John—unreal highs when they made love and the deep, abiding hurt she felt when he ignored her around his racing friends? Or the excruciating fear that creeped up her legs to her chest when John had taken unnecessary chances? There was no consistency with him, just highs and lows in abundance.

So, what did she want? She thought she knew. She wanted a man who would be a constant in her life. Someone she could depend on who wasn't reckless or overly aggressive—always having to prove a point.

Roarke scared her. She wanted a man who was guided by her needs as much as his own. And that wasn't Roarke, she thought sourly.

Tears involuntarily slipped from her blue-green eyes, tears that had taken years to finally come to the surface and fall in rivulets down her face, dripping off one at a time onto her lap. At least Roarke had made her cry again. Not from happiness, but from the realization that she was alone and could possibly spend the rest of her life alone unless she learned how to give more than she expected in return. Could she give to Roarke without always worrying about losing him when he didn't respond as she thought he should? The thought depressed her. Would she fall in love with him if she wasn't careful? No!

The frantic activity at the Yong Dong Pō site the next morning was refreshing after a quiet, lonely evening in her apartment. Workers were busy moving in bulldozers and bundles of bamboo poles to construct a temporary barrier around the site until the chain-link fence could be erected.

Curious people already were gathering at the site to watch—among them a truant Myune, still carrying his paper bag loaded with undelivered *Morning Suns,* Seoul's English-language newspaper.

"Myune!" she shouted.

A startled Myune looked as if he would bolt, but he waited for Clover to approach, a guarded expression on his face.

"What're you doing here?" she asked.

"Watching," he said, lowering his head.

"School started a half-hour ago and you haven't even delivered your papers yet!"

"I watch Roarke. He's good, Clover. A real man!"

Oh yeah, she thought. Macho down to his underwear. "He didn't get that way neglecting his work and school," she admonished.

"Nagging the poor kid again?" Roarke's words inflamed her anger. She turned, flashes of fire leaping from her eyes.

"He's late for school," she said. "He can't afford to miss it. He's way behind."

"The kid's curious. Let him watch." Roarke's chin stuck out in defiance of Clover's rule over the child.

"Oh, boy!" Myune dropped his paper bag and sat on it.

"No way." Clover took Myune by the arm and pulled him up. "Off!" She pointed toward school. "I'll take care of your papers. Now, go!"

Myune looked at Roarke, appealing to him with innocent eyes.

Clover stared at Roarke equally hard, daring him to cross her over Myune.

"I think you'd better go, chum. Some other day you can stay."

Myune sighed, looked accusingly at Clover, and walked off as slowly as he could without getting into more trouble.

"Tell your teacher I'll talk to her later in the day about this," Clover called after Myune.

"Okay," he answered, not turning around to look at her.

Pivoting angrily back to Roarke, Clover said between clenched teeth, "Myune started school a year later than other kids his age. He'll never catch up if he misses even a day. Please, don't try to undermine my authority with him, too. It's so tenuous anyway."

"Do you realize your eyes flash when you're mad?"

Roarke's sensuous smile made her shiver in response. Damn him, she thought. She looked down to avoid his eyes and found her gaze focused on the open throat of his plaid shirt. Mesmerized, her eyes passed the springy wedge of exposed black curls as her glance continued toward his belt and down to his jeans, stretched tight across his thighs. She felt heat begin to flush her cheeks.

Roarke returned her intense gaze as if he knew what she was feeling. He smiled again. It was a warm, loving smile that she needed right now.

"Maybe I shouldn't be so skeptical, Clover. But you're creating a monster by giving Myune a private-school education. He's with kids way out of his class. What's it going to be like for him after? They'll shun him, and people of his own class will be afraid of him."

"I'll take care of that! Myune will do all right."

"You always have to have the last word, don't you, Clover?" Roarke turned and walked away. She watched him; a furious need to shout back at him died in her throat. Then she realized she couldn't just let him walk away. She needed him. Myune needed him. It was important to her to win Roarke over regarding the boy.

"Roarke?" she called.

But he turned, waved, and kept on walking.

Clover felt a stab of misgiving. My God, she wondered, is this going to be an up-and-down love affair, with me doing the ups and downs? Then she remembered that there was no affair, no relationship, no love, and that she had better understand that. Angrily, she picked up Myune's paper bag and walked off toward his school to talk to his teacher.

Clover knew as she walked rapidly that Roarke's ever-present place in her professional life would create intolerable problems for her and she would have to slowly ease him out of her way. What a terrible mistake she had made going to Cheju Dō with him.

It wasn't until that evening, after a day filled with tension over Myune and her ongoing quarrel with Roarke, that Clover was able to relax in her apartment with a cup of tea.

The age-old conflict of man versus woman had made her prickly and determined to prove her worth. For thousands of years the Korean culture had viewed women as useful tools rather than people with feelings and needs. As a woman's usefulness declined, she was shunted aside for youth. However, ironically, it was age and not youth that was venerated here. So whatever a woman's age, she found that the superficial desires of men dictated her status.

As modern as Mr. Hwang and his friends were, they still adhered to the old beliefs. Why else did they continue the Kisang tradition? A Kisang girl was the embodiment of a subservience that bolstered the male ego almost to the point of godliness.

Clover felt a knot of anger—one that sometimes choked her when she dealt with the advisory committee. She kept her calm as much as possible, but there were times, as in Cheju Dō, when she overreacted. She did not regret giving Roarke hell for his tantrum over her hunting prowess, but she had, all the same, denied his very real concern over Mr. Hwang's and the other men's reaction to her insistence on being treated as an equal and ordering Roarke around after the party.

The question of Myune also posed difficulties for her. He had become her indirect responsibility since Mrs. Kaeng had, through no fault of her own, taken little interest in him. Now Roarke was suggesting she should not provide for him. What business was it of his? she asked herself. Or perhaps he was only trying to help? The confusion of their relationship had been doubly compounded by Myune's life in a netherworld of poverty and ignorance.

The next day and the days that followed, when her life became a blur of activity, she kept the problem alive in her mind, cautiously avoiding conflict and intensely aware of the needs of the men she dealt with—including Myune's. It was a delicate balance for one woman to maintain. But she vowed that no matter how tense or busy she was, she wouldn't allow Roarke to provoke her into a confrontation. After all, she realized, he had his problems, too.

She was forced to spend more and more time with Roarke as the days lurched by—twelve-hour days that were as professionally rewarding as any she could remember. But she also felt, in spite of her resolutions, a deep personal need that Roarke had aroused on Cheju

Dō. When she saw him away from the office her foolish heart chased after him—only to be greeted by his quicksilver smile and a wave. In the office they confined their conversation to the job. Her professional sense told her to drop him from her personal life. Since he had thrown himself heart, body, and soul into the project, she felt she should be able to sever more easily the emotional bond he had placed around her heart. But she could not.

On top of her hectic schedule, Clover began to worry more about Myune. He had become more difficult to keep in school because he wanted to be with Roarke—the pathetic need of a lonely little boy to be with his idol.

However, one time Prince Yee had taken Myune's hand to lead him away from the site when Roarke was too busy to watch him. Myune almost froze. Prince Yee was the pretender to the throne of Korea and, had it not been for the Japanese invasion and two wars, would indeed be king at this moment. Even in modern-day Korea, a poor schoolboy didn't hold the king's hand! Myune had excitedly told Clover about it and then rushed off to school to tell his friends. When Clover talked to the prince about Myune's reactions, he became very serious.

"You are giving him a good education," he said, hesitating. "But I wonder, Clover, if it is good for him?"

"You sound like Roarke. He said almost the same thing. What's wrong with a bright child getting a good start in life?"

"Nothing. I just think he will eventually need more. Are you prepared for that?"

"More?"

"Yes. He is bright and very handsome. I would like to see him given a chance to use that intelligence and education when he grows up. If you ever need my help with him, please ask."

"I will, sir. Thank you," she answered, puzzled.

So maybe Roarke was right, she thought. But she

could no more withdraw her care and concern for Myune's schooling than she could her love. She loved the boy—perhaps too much. Someday a decision about his future would be made, but by whom was questionable. Legally she had no claim on him, so the government would have to step in. Then what?

Clover despaired, her head pounding from the ominous possibility that Myune might not be her little boy one day. With that depressing thought, Clover threw herself into the project, working as furiously as Roarke. Maybe she could forget them both. Myune and Roarke? She knew she could not.

On a Monday morning, after having worked two straight weeks without a day off, Roarke suddenly appeared in Clover's doorway.

"Can I come in?" he asked.

Clover was surprised to see him, at least see him standing still, leaning against the jamb.

"Come in and sit down," she said quietly, her heart pounding in her chest and bringing on the flush of warmth that only Roarke could send through her.

"I wanted to apologize to you about Myune. He shows up every morning at the site and I have to chase him away. Finally I sat down with him a minute and talked to him about delivering his papers on time and getting to school. I hope it helped."

Clover told him about her conversation with Prince Yee.

"I feel the same as he does. Myune can't live his entire childhood in a pauper's shack, torn between you, and me, and school. He needs more . . . but what can we do? He has that old woman and the law says a child has to live with his nearest relative. Otherwise the orphanages would overflow with unwanted kids."

Clover sat quietly. She hadn't wanted to face the problem about Myune's future just yet. She kept hoping it would work itself out. But now that fragile future was being questioned, and one day she would have to face the possibility of losing another child.

Maybe she and Roarke . . . As quickly as the thought came to her she pushed it away. Roarke had never made overtures about the future and never would. She reminded herself that Roarke lived only for today and was dangerous to her well-being.

"Hey. We'll do what we can, Clover. Don't worry before it's necessary," he said, smiling at her in an understanding way that gave her momentary hope. Both of them had attached some emotional piece of their lives to Myune, who in turn was torn between them.

"Now, about Cheju Dō. How can I make it up to you?" he asked, giving her his best boyish grin. "I want to apologize for my nasty disposition and try again."

Clover held her hand up and said, "I think I should apologize to you. The situation called for tact, but I chose to fight instead. We both have to make our way here and by helping each other I know we can. I'm trying to say I'm the one who's sorry." Clover had rehearsed that speech for weeks and it still came out as if she had read it. But it was said, and whether Roarke realized it or not, she meant it.

"I have to go to Hong Kong for some equipment," he said.

Hong Kong! It was her favorite city next to San Francisco. In fact, it reminded her of San Francisco—the hills, the bay, the bustling streets. Hong Kong. The Magic City. It had been years since she'd been there.

"Are your beautiful eyes saying you'd like to go, too?"

Clover regretted her vow of no more Roarke. "I can't afford the time. Sorry."

"I have an emergency meeting with my partner. And we need a pump that we can only get in Hong Kong. It would take six weeks to get it from Taiwan. Why don't you come along? Let me make up for my bad manners."

Clover knew she would say yes; so why not just say it? she asked herself. "All right. I guess I can find the time. Thank you. And you've apologized quite enough."

Roarke grinned. "We'll take off Wednesday morning. The Peninsula Hotel, all right?"

"The Peninsula? Really?" Clover was astonished. "How did you get reservations at the Peninsula? They're booked six months in advance."

"My Hong Kong office keeps rooms there. It impresses clients," he said, his dark eyes reflecting his amusement.

Roarke stood up and walked behind Clover's desk. He leaned down and whispered in her ear. "I'll expect Scheherazade to come with me. After all, Hong Kong is a licentious city—there are sinful things to do there."

Clover felt a shudder ripple through her body like an earthquake. Roarke's lips ran carnal trails from her ears to her mouth. Capturing her in his arms, he lifted her from her chair and began a hard, demanding campaign to bring her to a sexual pitch that she had tried to suppress during the last few weeks.

"If I had gotten this close to you after we began site prep, we would still be in the first phase of the project. I had to avoid being too friendly if I was going to get anything done." Roarke's wild tongue began to tease her mercilessly. "Forgive me?" he asked.

He didn't let her answer, but continued his assault on her nervous system, his arms encircling her body, his fingertips reaching around to her breasts, caressing them until they were firm and responding wantonly.

Suddenly a throbbing need boiled up in her and she cried out in a small, uncertain voice, "Roarke, I need you."

"I know, Clover. I need you, too. We're good for each other."

No call for love. She desperately needed love. But love was still that elusive sylph, flitting invisibly around them, tempting them, but never within reach.

"We'll have to wait," he said suddenly. "I don't think your office is secure enough for what I have in mind. Wednesday? Hong Kong?" he whispered.

The siren call. Roarke knew exactly what it took. A magical few days in a mystical city, in a hotel fit for kings. Victoria Peak. The New Territories. The Star Ferry. All a few hours away, and she couldn't wait.

They landed at Kai Tek Airport in Hong Kong late Wednesday morning. Clover shut her eyes as the jet sailed in over the harbor, seemingly headed for either a dunk in the bay or a crash into the hills at the other end. Only when the familiar squeal of tires on the runway and the reverse thrust of the jet engines brought the plane to a fast stop did she open her eyes. Roarke was watching her, laughing.

"Kai Tek is no airport to land at if you don't like thrills."

"I understand pilots find it equally exciting," she shot back good-naturedly.

They filed obediently off the plane and into customs. Roarke's partner, a ruddy-looking Englishman, whisked them through the formalities, then to a waiting Peninsula Hotel Rolls Royce, shining in the brilliant sun that greeted them as they emerged from the noisy terminal building.

"Clover, this is my partner, Sid Neff, who runs our Hong Kong office. Sid, this is Clover McBain, my Seoul partner on the Yong Dong Pō project." Roarke laughed at his pun.

Sid leaned over in the back seat of the chauffeured Rolls and shook her hand. His thick, almost exaggerated British accent seemed quite in place.

"Clover," he said. "Roarke didn't tell me that C.S. McBain was a gorgeous bird. Welcome to the colony. Been here before, have you?"

"Yes. Twice, several years ago. Nice to meet you, Sid."

Sid gave Roarke an envious glance, then settled back

in the seat and began a nonstop monologue on several of the Hong Kong projects they were involved in.

Clover leaned back in the sumptuous gray Silver Shadow that glided silently through the maze of streets to the exquisite hotel five miles from Kai Tek. The Peninsula Hotel is one of the last of a dying breed—the Grand Hotel. Fit for kings, dukes, presidents, secret agents, and another dying breed, the romantic. Clover placed herself in this last category.

They slithered up to the marble entrance, red-carpeted and awesome with its white marble temple dogs guarding the doors, where a bevy of white-suited bellboys, captains, and assorted helpers descended on them, refusing to allow them to carry even a small case.

Clover had never been in the Peninsula, but in all her imaginings she had not come close to its elegant grace. A Coromandel screen, painted during the Ch'ing Dynasty in the late seventeenth century, greeted them. Clover had seen its mate in the Metropolitan Museum of Art in New York.

It wasn't necessary to check in, so they were led directly to their two adjoining rooms. The decor in the rooms was as opulent as the lobby's, precious Oriental art splashed in a well-ordered but casual manner throughout. A small page boy about Myune's age came in with jasmine tea in exquisite china. As Clover, Roarke, and Sid relaxed over the tea, another white-uniformed boy came in with a tray of luxury French soaps for Clover to choose for her baths. Hard on the heels of the soap came a half-dozen arrangements of fresh flowers in vases that Clover would have sinned for.

"Service is good here," Roarke said, winking at Sid.

"Good? It's spooky," she whispered.

Sid interrupted. "I made reservations at Gaddi's for tonight and the Marco Polo for tomorrow night. Hope that's okay."

"Fine," Roarke said, looking at Clover, who nodded her head in agreement.

"Let's leave Clover so she can freshen up and start her shopping." Roarke stood up and smiled down at Clover. "I want to check the equipment this afternoon, in case it isn't what we want. Then there'll be time to make changes."

Sid and Roarke waved good-bye to Clover. After they left she rushed into the bathroom to take a bath with the fragrant soap she had chosen.

Her bath finished, Clover sped downstairs and out the door. The doorman hailed a taxi for her and she gave the driver the address of a well-known dressmaker. She had a picture of an expensive Galanos beaded gown in her purse and she intended to have it copied for a fraction of the cost of the genuine one. After that, she would buy shoes from Lee Kee and visit several antique shops for vases and dishes. That would take up the rest of the day and still give her time to get ready for dinner with Roarke.

That evening, tired but satisfied with her day's shopping, she sank into a chair in her room to wait for Roarke. For the last month hardly a day had gone by without being with him, either running down the street in Yong Dong Pō beside him, watching him work at the site, or grabbing a bite to eat at Mr. Yun's shop. She realized that for the few hours she spent without him today she missed him terribly, and now welcomed his company, even if they were in formal dress and not alone.

A quiet knock at the door made her jump up in anticipation. She answered it and saw Roarke grinning at her.

"Hi, love." Before Clover could react to the word "love," which Roarke seemed to use so casually, he introduced her to Sid's wife.

"This is Liesl Neff, Sid's outrageously beautiful wife.

Don't you think she's much too lovely for him?" Roarke teased.

Liesl's German accent was as thick as Sid's British one. Together they made a charming couple. Sid was medium height, with sandy-blond hair and a ruddy complexion that he later explained were from his Scottish ancestors. Liesl was a petite woman with almost white-blond hair, deep blue eyes, and a china-doll skin that glowed as if she had a light on inside of her. She was as charming and nice as she was pretty. Next to the tall, commanding Roarke, Sid and Liesl looked like two dolls.

Gaddi's, Clover had read, was one of the world's best restaurants, and her anticipation was rewarded by its splendor. Their table had five waiters who did nothing but see to the comfort and service of the guests. They hovered, they served, and they worried over the four of them. The maître d'hôtel made a creamy lemon sauce for chicken called *beurre maître d'hôtel,* the most famous dish in this incredible restaurant. It was served along with Iranian caviar, fine wines from the private cellars of France's great chateaux, and a flawless flaming dessert. The same spooky service that prevailed throughout the hotel was haunting them here. A used fork was invisibly whisked away to be replaced by another, a sip of water from a crystal glass brought a refill without anybody realizing it. Every movement any of them made was answered immediately and uncannily by these waiters.

When the elegant theatrics of the maître d'hôtel drew to a close and their dinners were set before them, Liesl Neff turned her innocent blue eyes on Roarke.

"Sid and I have been anxiously waiting for you to finally bring one of your women to meet us. We knew when you did she'd be the one. Am I right, Roarke?"

It was all Clover could do to keep a noncommittal smile on her face. Sid was apoplectic. But Liesl apparently knew what she was doing.

"You know, Clover," Liesl said, winking across the table, "you'll have your hands full with this one—literally."

Roarke's deeply tanned face turned an intense red.

Liesl's eyes danced in pure enjoyment as she leaned back in her chair to watch Roarke's face turn crimson.

"Liesl, for God's sake . . ." Sid hissed out of the corner of his mouth.

Clover reached for her wine glass. Roarke tried to clumsily change the conversation, but Liesl would have none of it.

"We always want Roarke to stay longer when he comes to Hong Kong. But he seems to be continually running—to or from something. I don't know. Clover," she said in a throaty voice, "you'll get him to slow down, won't you? Why don't you talk him into staying over a few more days?"

"I'd love to stay but we have the project to get back to. It's in the critical stage right now and even these few days away are more than we can afford." Clover watched Sid, who had beat the solicitous waiter to the wine bottle, pour a full measure for Roarke.

"By the way, Roarke, Monique keeps asking me about you. For a short time I thought she had a chance. But of course, after meeting Clover I can see why she was just another of your passing fancies." Liesl reassured Clover, "A local girl he met at one of our parties."

Clover managed an outward calm but her insides were fluttering. She knew what Liesl was trying to do, but she knew also that Roarke couldn't be pushed.

"I haven't been to the People's Republic of China yet. Have you?" It was Clover now who tried to change the subject. Poor Roarke. She smiled as she gulped down the wine. The slightly piqued waiter jumped quickly to refill her glass.

"Actually," Liesl said before Sid or Roarke could interject, "we were all planning to go to China during

Roarke's last visit, but something happened between him and—"

"Liesl, have more wine," Sid interrupted as he and the waiter vied for the bottle while the sommelier ran up to their table with a bottle of champagne to replace the wine they had all drunk down as if it were a common table variety, "and shut up," he finished.

The whole drama acted out between Sid and the waiter while Liesl carried on a one-woman boxing match with them was becoming so funny that Clover was ready to violate the hush-hush atmosphere of Gaddi's by laughing out loud. Then the absolutely unthinkable happened.

The sommelier tripped over Liesl's carelessly placed purse and popped the champagne cork too hard. The cork flew up and over the room like a well-aimed missile, landing in the dessert of a stuffy-looking older woman, whose sour expression deepened. For a moment the entire scene was still—waiters and patrons alike froze in horrible anticipation.

Clover watched the old woman, elegant in an elaborately coiffed hair style and a beaded dress, pick the cork out of her mousse, stand as regally as a queen, and walk over to the shocked sommelier.

"I believe, Tom, this is yours," she said, dropping the cork into his pocket and walking in slow, measured steps back to her table. All five of her waiters scrambled to seat her.

Clover could stand the strain no more, and burst out laughing. Liesl joined her as Sid and Roarke frowned, and the two women kept up a side-splitting laugh while the other patrons tried to suppress their own guffaws. A few snorted but most just grinned. Poor Tom, the sommelier, handed the opened bottle of champagne to a waiter and disappeared to die a little in private.

After she had calmed down, still wiping tears from her face, Liesl patted Roarke on the cheek. "Don't be a stuffed shirt. If you let her go, I'll personally haunt you wherever you are. Stop and smell the flowers, Roarke, my sweet. If you don't you'll regret it for the rest of your life."

Roarke reached over, his fist balled up, and gave Liesl a gentle, affectionate sock on the jaw.

They finished the meal in a semblance of calm, with Clover and Liesl punctuating the ambience with quiet bursts of occasional laughter. They finally rose, tipped the staff generously, and left.

As they said their good-byes in the lobby, the old woman whose dessert was interrupted by the flying cork appeared behind them. She pointed a long, thin finger at Clover.

"Young lady," she spoke solemnly, "I wish to have a word with you." Imperiously, she walked toward Clover.

Clover felt like Anne Boleyn being approached by the headsman. "Yes, ma'am," she stuttered.

"I must say, in my years dining at Gaddi's, I've never enjoyed myself more. I dine alone every night without a single person to talk to. Tonight was the highlight of my week. Poor Tom, of course, failed to see the humor, but I spoke to the management to assure he'll continue as sommelier."

Clover smiled in relief. "It was terribly funny. I'm glad you realized we weren't laughing at you."

The old woman smiled back and Clover could see the remnants of a truly beautiful face from beneath the wrinkles.

"In fact, I'm going back to my rooms and have a good laugh over some Drambuie." With that the old woman turned and walked away.

Clover watched her and her heart cried out. To be old and lonely, no matter how rich, could seem like the end of the world. What did someone once say? Loneliness is everything it's cracked up to be. She felt tears sting her eyes as the old woman disappeared around a corner.

"My God," Sid gasped. "Now I know who she is. She's a Russian refugee. The Czar's young cousin, Countess somebody or other. Holy cow."

They all laughed and said their good-byes once more.

"Remember what I told you, Roarke," Liesl said as Sid dragged her away.

Sated and unable to move very fast, Roarke and Clover had an after-dinner drink on the verandah, sipping a liqueur that tasted like ambrosia but was acting more like an aphrodisiac. Roarke grinned over the rim of his glass and then put it down. He stood up and extended his hand.

"Let's go. I can't wait for you any longer. These last celibate weeks, after tasting the wine of desire, were agony."

"You sound like a poet." She laughed.

"I mean it, Clover. You gave me a taste of something that I can't live without now."

She studied his eyes for a sign that he really meant "the rest of his life." The sparkle was there, but she still couldn't read him.

She gave him her hand and let him lead the way to the elevator that, of course, magically opened the moment they stepped in front of it. The lift boy smiled as he shut the door and silently took them to the third floor. Roarke had wrapped his large hand around hers and held it tight, as if he feared letting go would cause her to disappear.

They walked silently to her room. Roarke pulled out a key and unlocked the door. He held it open for her to go through, shutting it firmly behind them. A red rose lay on her pillow and a basket of fresh tropical fruits stood on the stand nearby.

Roarke picked up the rose and brushed it against her cheek.

"For the woman who makes my life worthwhile. Liesl recognized how I feel about you." He handed the rose to her.

He was everything she thought she wanted and wondered if he could ever commit himself to more than snatches of love in Cheju Dō and Hong Kong.

"Thinking stops action. You're thinking too much. Come here." His seductive voice called to her and his hand reached out possessively. "Come here so I can do what I wanted to do that day in your office." She felt herself propelled toward him, unable to stop the wild fling of her heart in her chest.

His mouth came down on hers, demanding and needful, and she tasted the sweet ambrosia they had been drinking minutes before. His tongue plundered her mouth, making her forget any modesty she may have had.

His hands reached for the zipper on her dress and in seconds it was undone and falling around her feet in a blue cloud. Roarke deftly unhooked her bra and his mouth moved to her breasts, his tongue searing her nipples that had hardened from his touch.

Roarke then moved slowly with her to the bed, his hands and tongue exploring and probing. She fell to the bed with him in sinful pleasure as he tugged at her lace panties. When they were gone, she realized she was undressed and Roarke fully clothed. She fumbled with his tie and shirt.

"I was wondering when you would take the initiative." He laughed.

"Just hold still," she scolded gently.

She wanted him so badly she was shaking. He helped her unbutton his shirt and then stood to let his tuxedo trousers slide to the floor.

Roarke slid back into the bed with her and began to caress her again, working her into a frazzle of desire. She scraped her fingernails lightly across his back, feeling his muscles ripple in response.

"You'll get into trouble doing that." He pulled her even closer to him and planted a scorching kiss on her in a gesture that hovered between tenderness and savagery. She slumped against him in a surrender that made Roarke more possessive and demanding. She could not react with the intensity that she wanted to, so weak had she become under Roarke's tender assault. She growled at him. "Love me, damn you, before I pass out."

Roarke threw his head back and laughed. "The cool Young Ni!"

Clover did react this time by pushing him away. "Am I some kind of challenge? Now that Young Ni has given in, you're ready for something else?"

Roarke's eyes darkened. "You are touchy, aren't you? Of course I didn't mean that. I want to dispel the ghosts of your past; that's my goal. When I finally do that, then I'll have the woman I really want."

Clover felt her eyes sting from the tears that were building up behind them. "I want you so much that I fight every shadow that threatens me," she said. "You have ghosts, too. Some of them are so elusive that I don't know what to think about you."

"Hey. I'm just a man who is fast falling in love with a beautiful, fiery woman. Give us time. Don't expect me to see the light just yet. I'm scared, Clover. Of commitments, of love, of staying in one place too long."

She buried her face in his neck and then on impulse began biting him gently.

All of their control quickly slipped away. With urgent fury, Roarke rained kisses on her from her forehead to her toes. Their lovemaking would be even better, she knew, the longer she was forced to wait for him. And wait she did. While Roarke tortured her with slow, lingering kisses and bites, she ran her fingers through his hair, felt the strong muscles of his back and thighs, and tasted the sweet wine of his kisses.

"Clover, Clover. Sweet Clover, beautiful Scheherazade, quiet, thinking Young Ni. Who are you?" he whispered, almost as if he was afraid to find out who all of these women were, hiding in one tall, willowy strawberry-blonde, whose eyes threw sparks across the room when she was angry.

"Now, Clover. Now!" He growled at her, pushing her back and plunging into her with a furious desire that she matched.

The long, pulsating rhythm of desire reached a crescendo, and they peaked together in a quiet, urgent cry that echoed around them.

They lay still, hoping the night would never end. Sleep came, but it was periodically interrupted by strong hands around her or the sweet kisses that she planted on his smiling and vulnerable face as he slept. Throughout the night, they awakened with each other's love and desire. By morning they were deep in an intense sleep, when the phone rang.

It jangled until Roarke stirred, lifted the receiver, and groaned into it. Only after Clover was awake did she realize it was her phone that Roarke was sleepily answering in the early morning.

7

He mumbled into the receiver, "Roarke Devereaux, here," then lay back on the bed, rubbing his eyes. "Yes, I'll accept the call . . . Betty? . . . Uh, well, all the rooms are under my name." An imperceptible smile wavered on his lips, then disappeared. "If you want to talk to Clover, I'll go get her," he said, keeping up a facade of decorum that Clover appreciated.

She looked quizzically at Roarke, whose soft grunts punctuated long silences while he listened to Betty.

"What's wrong?" His voice cracked with disbelief. "A Buddhist priest? What the hell for?"

A momentary stab of panic swept through her. Had something happened to Myune?

"Look, Betty, I'll be back on the noon plane. Yeah," he snorted. "Don't worry. 'Bye." He hung up and let out an exasperated sigh.

"What is it, Roarke?" she asked. "What's happened?"

He made no reply. Did she imagine it, or had he

detached himself from her? A small, unreasonable prickle of annoyance touched her briefly. If something was wrong with their project or Myune, it was her concern, too.

"Well?" She felt herself becoming impatient with his silence. "Are you going to tell me what Betty said?"

With deliberate casualness belying the deep frown that drew his eyebrows together and tightened his jaw, he turned to her. "Seems the men at the site stopped work. They've called in a Buddhist priest."

"Why would they want a Buddhist priest if it's a work stoppage?"

"Beats me."

He abruptly reached out and slapped Clover on her bottom, "Holiday's over," he said, laughing.

She was unsure if she should take offense at his sudden gesture. She regarded his face warily, then realized that his action had been perfectly normal as the tension of his hand changed to a soft caress, pressing gently into her willing flesh—a prelude to yet more lovemaking.

At that point Clover impulsively turned the tables on him. She reached over and slapped him on the bottom.

"Hey, old boy, we have a plane to catch, remember?" Laughing, she rolled out of bed and padded to the bathroom. She glanced briefly over her shoulder to see Roarke scoop his clothes up off the floor and head for his room, an expression of utter male bewilderment branded on his face.

Clover was rather pleased with herself as she walked into the bathroom and shut the door firmly behind her. Then memories of the night before flooded back and a pure, female joy erupted from her. The searing kisses Roarke freely gave her, and her eager willingness to take them, devour them, and beg for more had crumbled every defense, every wall she had carefully built to protect herself from being hurt again.

She stepped into the shower and turned on the cold water. She hated cold showers, but they revived her when she needed it most. The force of the water drummed against the nerve endings in her tired body, bringing her back to the reality that the "holiday" was indeed over. She and Roarke would have to face together whatever problem they found at the site. She lathered, rinsed, and toweled herself dry. Shivering from the cold air, she dressed in a serviceable cotton blouse, khaki pants, and the new boots she had picked up at Lee Kee's the day before.

She dumped her clothes willy-nilly into the suitcase, then kicked the top of the case closed with her foot. Hurriedly she wrote a note to the hotel manager asking him to instruct the dressmaker to mail her dress to her when it was finished. By the time she had completed her chores, Roarke was coming through the door with his luggage.

"The bellboy's on the way up. Just leave your luggage here; he'll get it."

She leaned over, locked her suitcase, and followed Roarke to the elevator.

"Damned intriguing," he said as the elevator descended slowly. Then he changed the subject entirely, throwing her completely off balance.

"Clover, why don't you stay behind a few days and finish your shopping?"

For some absurd reason her mind teetered with doubt.

"Why?" she asked bluntly. "Are we afraid of what we'll find?"

His jaws clearly clenched and his face shuttered closed. "It might avoid a lot of grief if you don't come back with me."

An awkward tension kept them from talking for a few minutes.

"Stop it, Roarke. You know as well as I do that a tomb may have been discovered at the site."

He buried his face in her hair and whispered, "I'm not ready for this. I didn't want conflict in our lives right now. Stay behind here," he coaxed. "I'll handle it alone."

"No." She resolutely stood her ground. "It's my project, too. I want to face the beast straight-on."

"Suit yourself, damn it."

"Yes, Roarke, I will this time. It's a matter of principle."

"Your rules on love and life are sometimes too progressive for me," he said, his voice barely above a whisper. "For once I'd like you to be compliant."

"Never," she whispered back. "I had enough of that with John."

After they landed at Kimpo Airport in Seoul and cleared customs, they walked out to the front of the terminal building.

"Coming to the site with me?" His question was cautious.

"No, thanks. I want to get back to my office first."

Roarke hailed a cab. "Not quite up to it?" He opened the cab door and grinned at her. "The beast, I mean?"

She smiled back at him—a grim, ironic smile. She wanted to get into the cab with him and end the pounding tension that had built between them. No man had ever affected her like Roarke—not even John, she realized now. It frightened and moved her, too. She needed to touch Roarke—to pull his energy and life through to her body. But she stopped. An opposite reaction was also tugging at her. As anxious as she was to see the construction area, she thought it would be better to talk to Betty about what had happened first. She watched the cab drive him away.

She steadied herself and hailed the next cab in line. But she did not ride in it alone. Roarke's presence pervaded her senses, and as hard as she tried to ignore it, it lingered on—the ache to be with him, the longing and the tension.

She half ran up the back stairs to her office on the fifth

floor. The clacking sound of Betty's typewriter was oddly reassuring, as if impending disaster didn't lurk in the dark corners of her life. But the moment she pushed the reception room door open, Betty jumped up.

"Thank God you're back." Betty's harried frown creased her peaches-and-cream complexion and her honey-blonde hair looked as if she had been furiously running her long fingers through it all morning. Clover's stomach knotted.

Resolutely she stood firm, trying not to let her secretary's near hysteria touch her. "What happened, Betty?" Clover was surprised at her own calmness.

"This is Lee Han Ko, one of the workers at the site. Ko is also an archaeology student at the university. He's been here since morning, waiting for you," Betty blurted out.

The young Korean stood up and bowed to her. "It is so good you are back," he said. "I did not have the authority to call Doctor Lee, but I think we have uncovered the roof of a very ancient tomb, perhaps as old as Silla."

"That's what I thought when Roarke told me a Buddhist priest was consulted. When did it happen?"

"I do not know, exactly. We began to unearth large, rounded pieces of river rock yesterday. But because we are close to the river, no one thought much about it. And, no mound was evident, so of course the thought of a possible tomb did not occur to me." The student spoke in precise but halting English.

"And?"

"As we dug deeper, it was finally evident that the rocks formed a rectangle about one hundred feet long and fifty feet wide. Perhaps, it's the roof of a royal tomb. A corner of it collapsed this morning when a bulldozer ran over it. I peered into the hole but could see only more rock. Nothing to assure me it was a tomb. It could be the foundation of an old building," he finished.

"What did you say to the workers?" she asked, turning to the phone on Betty's desk and picking up the receiver.

"I speculated, but nothing was really evident . . ."

"That was all you needed to do to get the workers to stop clearing the debris away."

Clover wrangled with the operator on the phone in an attempt to locate Doctor Lee at the university.

The student-worker continued, "Another worker ran to the temple down the street and summoned the priest. I left the site to come here, and have been here since."

Suddenly Clover heard Jin-Soo's voice on the other end of the phone and she jumped to life. "Jin-Soo? I'm back. Something has been unearthed at the project site." Clover waited. "Yes," she answered. "One of your students thinks it might be . . . Will you come? . . . I'd appreciate it . . . Should I call Prince Yee? Thank you."

She hung up. "Doctor Lee will call Prince Yee and then come here before we go to the site together." Clover tapped her fingers on the desk. Patience had never been one of her virtues.

It was a long, agonizing thirty minutes before Jin-Soo Lee arrived, out of breath. He, too, was tense with excitement. Clover could see the muscles in his jaw flex, and his eyes narrowed at her as he walked in. She couldn't read him. He was masking the emotions that he felt. Her heart pounded in her throat and she swallowed hard to make it stop.

After what seemed like minutes, Jin-Soo dragged his eyes from her and turned to Ko, questioning him sharply about the discovery. Ko lowered his head and answered Doctor Lee in a barely audible voice.

Just as Jin-Soo finished, Prince Yee walked in, bringing with him a calm, authoritative air that settled over them like a cool breeze.

They exchanged quick, polite greetings. But Clover's elation fast returned to the nervous strain she had felt all day, when Jin-Soo hastily grabbed her arm and without his usual courtliness pulled her with him through the door. A deep scowl pinched his face as they walked down the stairs. Prince Yee, with Ko and Betty, followed. As Jin-Soo's fingers tightened around her arm, she felt herself mentally holding on to the sides of a roller coaster careening over a wild course.

Even the unusually placid street did nothing to control the incessant pounding in her temples and the distant rumble of a crowd merely reinforced her sense of disaster.

Feeling like Dorothy from *The Wizard of Oz,* Clover linked arms with Prince Yee and Jin-Soo and they marched three abreast down the gray-brick sidewalk toward the site.

The old buildings in various stages of destruction loomed ahead. Hundreds of curious faces turned to greet them. Their approach parted the crowd like a ship parts water, and they continued through, never slackening their pace. Jin-Soo's protective hand on her arm suddenly dropped away, and she saw the bizarre scene in front of her, a montage of action momentarily frozen in time.

The crowd that had formed beyond the flimsy fence was quiet, but beneath this surface calm Clover could feel the tension strung tightly, waiting to burst out in anger or confusion. For now, they held fast, watching in a peculiar fascination as the red light of a rescue truck provided the only sign that something was happening.

Prince Yee threaded his competent way toward Roarke, who was helping the rescue crew pick up a man from the ground near a tipped-over bulldozer and place him on a gurney. As soon as the rescue truck pulled away and left the site, the figures that had been standing deathly still, watching, began to move again. Prince Yee approached Roarke and asked him what had happened.

Roarke didn't answer right away, but looked apologetic and frustrated. "The bulldozer tipped over when another part of the roof caved in," he finally said. A strange lack of emotion made his voice seem hollow. His expression was tight; mixed feelings flickered then disappeared from his face. His concern for the injured worker and his anger simmered beneath the surface, ready to spill over.

He must have sensed Clover standing apart from the scene, watching him. She saw him turn his head a bit to look at her, as if she had deliberately planned the new neighborhood on top of a tomb. He must have known, of course, she would never have done that, and perhaps he was feeling a stab of regret that they had not had enough time for a deepening relationship to form before this conflict tested the strength of their beliefs—in life and each other.

But time had run out. Jin-Soo and Ko were kneeling down at the enormous hole in the corner of the tomb roof, nodding their heads in agreement.

Clover moved closer to Roarke. "Are you all right?"

"Yeah, but this whole damned project's been jeopardized."

Prince Yee interrupted. "Tell me, Roarke, what really happened. I cannot help if I know only half of it."

Roarke gave the prince a enigmatic look—bold yet wounded.

"It's all my fault," he began. "I lost track of the big picture. I made a thoughtless remark, saying we should cover the tomb up. Of course I wasn't serious but my foreman thought I was and ordered the workers to begin bulldozing dirt over the rocks. Before I could stop them, the bulldozer tipped over and injured the driver. The priest told the workers that their ancestors had risen up to smite them. After that, it was all downhill."

The prince patted Roarke on the shoulder. "Let me talk to the priest," he said, and walked away.

Roarke used his heavily booted foot to trace angry lines in the dust, his hands thrust deep into his jacket pockets, his eyes surveying the world around him—a world he was so determined to shape his way.

Clover moved in yet closer to Roarke. "I'm sorry, Roarke. We didn't need this."

"Yeah, so am I." He looked at her from under furrowed eyebrows. "Those poor river people have been waiting all of their lives for a decent and safe place to live. Contrary to what you believe, I admire your work; the way you take an empty lot, a piece of paper, and turn it into a whole new world. You designed a beautiful environment for them and I was going to make it work." He hesitated for a second. "I was going to make something else work, too. But this . . ." He threw a small rock at the roof of the tomb and stalked away.

She called after him. "Roarke. This isn't the end of the world. We can clear another area for them."

He turned. "When? Someday? They need it *now!*"

"Are you a quitter, Roarke Devereaux? One little obstacle and you throw your toys down and leave? The river people need a stronger champion than that." She was challenging everything he stood for and gambling it would bring him back.

Just at that point, the idiotic fervor that had taken hold of the city burst into life. Roarke stopped dead at the sight of news reporters and television cameramen frantically elbowing their way through the spectators, who by now had been shoved back to the sidewalk by the workers. Behind him the Buddhist priest stood accusingly alone by the tomb, his arms held aloft, his decorative robes billowing out like a high poonghie at a funeral. Roarke was trapped.

He turned around instantly and stalked back to Clover.

"So," he growled, "now we have the rabble-rousers on the scene. What next?"

"The mayor and General Han." She pointed to a limousine disgorging the mayor of Seoul and General Han.

Roarke swore softly and Clover tugged at his sleeve and pulled him toward some buildings that hadn't yet been torn down. "I have an idea. Let's talk over there."

Clover glanced over her shoulder at the absurd scene. She held back a nervous giggle—to her the show unfolding around the hole looked like a Laurel and Hardy comedy. But it wasn't the least bit funny. Down that hole, she knew, were the remains of some royal. But the artifacts buried with him would be the focus of all the energy Jin-Soo Lee could arouse in the populace. It would become *his* passion and obsession; she and Roarke would have to make theirs the re-creation of a year's hard work.

From this engulfing madness Roarke and Clover removed themselves unobstrusively. Anyway, she realized, they had been forgotten momentarily in the excitement, and no one would notice their absence. Roarke leaned against a wall, folded his arms, and waited for her to speak.

"They have to investigate it, you know, it's the law," Clover reminded him.

"I know," was his seemingly indifferent answer.

"Blast you!" she cursed. "I don't want that tomb there any more than you do."

"Please, don't lecture me, Clover. I'm aware of what's going to happen. Whenever there has to be a compromise, it's the poor whose lives are disrupted. I just didn't want them to be the victims this time."

"They won't be," she said softly. "We can bring in mobile homes for temporary housing and place them on that vacant land we had planned for a shopping center—the land near the edge of the district. The shopping center construction is years away anyhow."

Roarke narrowed his eyes. "You're still the most alive and beautiful woman I know."

Her nostrils flared and her breath came in short, fast gulps. She wanted to react appropriately, but the noise, not more than a hundred feet away, was a reminder of their public surroundings.

"Roarke," she admonished gently, "we're in the middle of a crisis."

"Uh-huh, and the crisis is really ours. Are we going to make it through all of that?" He waved his hand toward the fast-growing mob of onlookers.

"That depends on us, doesn't it? On whether we're mature enough to live with each other's ideas and principles?"

"I was hoping to avoid all that."

"All what? Conflict? Roarke, if it wasn't a royal tomb it would be something else. No two people can live their lives together without some kind of major clash."

"But clash over some despot's grave?" His eyes were angry, his smile gone. "No tomb," he hissed at her, "no matter who it belonged to, is worth people's lives."

"The Koreans care," she answered back, a bit louder than she had intended.

"The rich Koreans care. After all, only the rich had anything worth burying. Now the rich want the artifacts of the elite brought up to reinforce their sense of power and worth. To hell with the river-dwellers!"

Their voices became increasingly angry. "No! You're wrong!" Clover felt her blood rush to her cheeks. "It's the heritage of the whole country, not just a few."

Roarke straightened up. "Tell it to those people who live in shacks and are flooded out year after year. Tell them some cracked pot or trinket is worth more than they are."

"No, Roarke. You tell the people who line up to see the finds that their heritage isn't worth the effort!" Clover didn't really mean to sound so strident, but Roarke had precipitated the old argument of past versus future and she couldn't let it go by without challenging it.

Roarke stormed off, then stopped a few yards away. "Bring in your mobile homes. I'll get the land ready. It seems to be the only solution."

Clover watched Roarke walk toward the mayor and General Han. A proud, sensitive man, Clover reflected, who too often saw the world in black and white. She realized then how much he cared about the river-dwellers.

She looked around her, feeling a little lost. Jin-Soo was shining a spotlight into the hole. He had borrowed it from one of the local television stations that had sent a news team to the site. Roarke was talking to the mayor, and Prince Yee was giving one of his rare interviews.

The excitement eventually caught up with her. She walked briskly over to Jin-Soo and knelt down next to him. The odd feeling of an explorer about to discover something great aroused her. She rubbed her arm to make the trembling go away. "See anything?" She tried to smile eagerly at him but could only manage a foolish grin. However, it didn't matter. He was too engrossed with the hole to notice.

"Yes," he finally answered her. "Yes, I do! A heavy wooden beam that must form a corner support of the tomb. Remarkably, it is intact."

"Then it *is* a tomb?"

Jin-Soo looked surprised. "Of course; did you think it wasn't?"

"No, I guess not. It's just that . . . well . . . it does upset things here."

"I understand. What did you and Roarke decide about the river-dwellers? I saw you . . . uh . . . talking over by those buildings. We must not neglect the river people because of this discovery." It was not like Jin-Soo to

ct little boy. The papers were now delivered early
e got to school on time. Did that small child think he
d to atone for his normally rebellious behavior?
ome here, Myune!" she called to him. "Have some
."
poked his head in the door and smiled brightly.
he loved him!
ver, can I meet Doctor Lee? We all have to write
ay on the tomb. Can I?"
course. Want to walk to the site with me? I'll drop
f and then go on to see how Roarke is doing with
lers."
boy." He responded by throwing his arms
her.
so glad you came to see me first, Myune."
too. Can I have the candy?"
r burst out laughing and held the candy jar while
grabbed several pieces and stuffed them in his

walked to the site. Clover held the boy's hand
him through the gate, passing lines of students
ocks, and found Jin-Soo enthusiastically waving
oard around, directing the careful, meticulous
of debris from the deepening hole.
o? Can you spare a minute?" she called.
f course. Is this Myune?"
Myune. Myune, this is Doctor Lee."
e said shyly. "Can I watch what you're doing?"
's class has been assigned to write about the
vation," Clover explained. "Do you mind if he
ere and watches you?"
signaled to a student. "Find a hard hat for our
ue here."
eyes widened and he looked up at Clover.
ear him?" he whispered.
odded. "Do exactly what he says and stay
hole." She kissed him on the forehead, but

rattle on nervously, and Clover stared at him dumbfounded.

"Temporary mobile homes," she answered. "We have another site we can use."

"Good. Very good."

"How old is the tomb, do you think?" she asked.

"I cannot tell. From its location and condition it may be as old as Silla, I believe. But we'll see when we excavate."

"Roarke is upset," she blurted out.

"Yes. I think he would be." Jin-Soo turned his face to Clover. His small pencil moustache seemed too debonaire on his handsome face—a face now showing raw emotion.

He stood up. "I know how difficult this is for you. I only regret that we must disrupt your project. You have a fine mind, Young Ni. You must look for a new permanent site for the river-dwellers. This tomb—it cannot be compromised!" Jin-Soo spun around and walked away, conflicting emotions obviously tearing him apart.

Clover was so stunned that she remained on her hands and knees, staring into the black hole.

The din of the frenetic activity at the site had made her ears ring. But it was her heart that pounded in her head. As she made her way through the streets of Yong Dong Pō now, she hardly recognized the neighborhood—two weeks after the discovery. Hawkers had flooded the streets, shopkeepers had stocked extra commodities, and schoolgirls cleaned debris off the sidewalks to ready the district for the influx of tourists and sightseers. Clover wanted to reach the relative calm and security of her office, so she quickened her pace, pushing past food vendors and souvenir peddlers.

Jin-Soo had immediately mobilized the city's student population into a "volunteer" work force, hauling rocks, shoring up fragile beams, and arranging a large tent into an administrative center to catalogue any artifacts brought up. She had seen him begin an excavation before. He was efficient and dedicated.

His outburst had shaken her, making her feel light-headed and vulnerable. Nothing, it seemed, was right with her well-arranged world anymore. Relationships in this perplexing land were as fragile and unpredictable as the roof of an emperor's tomb, she decided. What could she possibly say or do now to assure Jin-Soo that she would find a new site for the river-dwellers, while she kept her love for Roarke on a steady course?

She sat at her littered desk, where she had begun an intense search for another suitable place to put the river-dwellers. The muted clicks of the computer keyboard as she punched in the information soothed her. At least she had something to keep her busy.

She studied the list of alternative sites that had been spewed out on several feet of computer paper. Deep inside of her a strange foreboding told her that it would be a long haul for everyone before life returned to normalcy.

Click. The computer kicked out another long sheet of statistics. Too bad, she thought, life's problems couldn't be solved on a computer readout. Push a button and the answers tumbled out. Push another button and alternatives to the first answers were presented.

She fingered the talisman that Jin-Soo had given her. Burning with fatigue, she pushed the computer sheets aside and laid her head on her folded arms. An aching desire to have a few hours alone with Roarke, away from all this madness, became a grand passion, throbbing somewhere deep inside her.

She felt a wholly sexual need for him. A convulsive sob spilled out and she raised her head to get a deep breath of air, listening for the familiar sounds of him in his office—Sam whining, a shuffled chair, anything! But only

quiet, lonely emptiness greeted her. Be
needed vacation and her temporary
come in today.

Clover pushed herself up from the
muscles were sore and her nerves r
over the computer for days, pulling o
on a new project site, and from the ke
write a long report for the adviso
needed to escape from it for awhile. J
Roarke and her spirits would be rene
of her mind and body.

She examined in minute detail h
who seemed to care so fiercely for
underdog. A truly compassionate n
was unable to show more than t
ments of his body and surface e
hell is Roarke Devereaux, anyw
Why couldn't she find the man
facade?

Dreamily pacing her office no
to run her fingers over the vas
her, or to examine her new ha
pretend she wasn't deeply, reck
—it was a self-destructive lo
ravage her mind and body un
She must tell Roarke, explai
upside-down world there wa
people to love and be alone

Coupled with her passio
sense of guilt. She had avoi
as an excuse not to get too
After all, she reassured hers
find a new site and adjust

A small voice bubbled c
source of her guilt. He h
tomb discovery. Both sh
neglected him, and he

perfe
and h
need
"C
candy
He
How
"Cl
an ess
"Of
you of
the tra
"Oh
around
"I'm
"Me,
Clove
Myune
pockets.
They
and took
hauling
his clipb
removal
"Jin-So
"Yes, o
"This is
"Hi," h
"Myune
tomb exca
sits over th
Jin-Soo
new collea
Myune's
"Did you h
Clover n
clear of the

Myune quickly wiped it away. "Don't kiss me in front of all the men," he whispered loudly. "They'll think I'm a sissy!"

Jin-Soo grinned at Clover over Myune's head and nodded. "He'll be fine. Are you staying? We're getting close to the actual burial area."

"I wish I could, but I have to see what's happening with the new trailers that came in. Maybe later. Thanks."

Trailers be damned! She wanted to see Roarke. Clover walked away. She turned to wave to Myune, but he was already engrossed in the excavation. It was Jin-Soo who stood looking after her, unsmiling and serious. He didn't wave back, but looked for a moment as if he would bolt after her. She knew he thought she should stay at the tomb. Nothing was more important to him; and her past enthusiasm had been a strong link between them.

But she had to see Roarke. Something inside of her demanded that. She was fast letting her desire for him turn into full-fledged love; but always it was tempered by an uneasiness that she couldn't explain.

The dream of love, not of being someone's—Roarke's—current plaything, drove her on. She shook her golden hair loose and let the humid air crinkle it up around her face in ringlets.

The gray-brick sidewalks showed signs of wear from millions of feet, both human and animal, that had trod down them daily since World War II and even before that time. Her breath was short and she paused to take air—air that might steady her nerves. How many lovers, she wondered, searched for their mates along these streets, often in vain because of the wars?

When she reached the trailer site she was breathless and much of her bravado had dissipated. It was one thing to announce bravely to yourself that you loved someone, but another to stand face-to-face with the man and tell him so, especially when you weren't sure whether he wanted to hear your fine and noble declarations.

Roarke was busy and looked perplexed as trailers were strewn catywampus over the site and workers all waited for his directions. She could hear him shouting in his roughest Korean—inflections he used only when he wanted to make sure his workers had no doubt of his intentions. She would have withered under such scathing orders, so she hesitated and backed away.

"Clover!" The familiar voice of Jin-Soo Lee came up behind her.

Startled, she turned abruptly to face him.

"What're you doing here?" she asked.

"Looking for you, of course. You should have stayed," he scolded. "We're there. We're at the casket—or almost. You can't miss being there when the first finds come up." Jin-Soo's face challenged her. "It's what we've all worked for, Clover."

Clover could only stare. "I can't . . . I mean . . ."

Jin-Soo looked sadly over her shoulder at Roarke. "What do you feel is more important? The discovery of the decade or a momentary visit to the trailer site?" He looked hard at her and a wave of indecision and guilt washed over her.

"The tomb . . . but I feel a responsibility."

"For what? Roarke seems in his own way to be handling the simple task of positioning the trailers. You'd be in the way."

"But," she stammered, then leaned against the building she had stopped in front of. "I'm so damned tired. You pull me one way, Roarke another, Myune another, and the advisory committee yet another. What do you all want from me?" She looked into Jin-Soo's eyes.

"The tomb. What else is there right now? I have to get back. Come with me, Clover. Roarke can wait."

Clover swayed. Jin-Soo steadied her. "Walk back with me," he urged gently. "I think you need some diversion right now."

She was unable at the moment to argue. She turned

her head to look once more at Roarke, who was too absorbed in his work to have noticed her.

As they walked back to the tomb, Clover wished she could snap her fingers and turn time back to the day Roarke first walked into her office. Things had been nice and simple then.

Neither Jin-Soo nor Clover spoke as they hurried to see the test hole that would determine if there were artifacts worth bringing up. When they reached the area, the crowd had quieted with tense anticipation.

It was an unlikely group that formed a circle around the entrance to the oblique hole that plunged over fifty feet into the middle of the burial site. Exposed beams, remarkably well-preserved for their age, formed a precise network of bearing walls for the tons of rock dumped over the site, making it impenetrable to all but the most aggressive grave-robbers.

Prince Yee, wearing Levi's and tee shirt, kneeled down near the edge of the hole, watching the student workers hand up one basketful of rocks at a time, while the Reverend Cho, the mayor, and General Han, all in three-piece suits, stooped down next to the prince. A few feet away Myune stood quietly, looking properly awed, next to several other boys his age who had gained privileged entry to the tomb site and were watching.

She gave each man the brightest smile she could and greeted them with an excitement in her voice that she began to feel in earnest now. Jin-Soo's face mirrored a tenseness that Clover could see was flowing through the crowd of onlookers. Imminent discovery had made her forget Roarke and the guilt she felt over her excitement that a tomb had been found in the middle of Yong Dong Pō.

A hush had fallen over everyone. Even the young students now handed the baskets up in reverential silence, as if they might disturb the sleeping royal below.

Clover took periodic deep breaths to alleviate the knot

inside of her and let her mind concentrate wholly on the excavation.

Suddenly the students froze, baskets suspended.

"There is something down here," cried a voice, muffled by distance.

The students came alive once more, handing up the baskets with a renewed fervor, until they slowly passed a basket along that held a precious object. Doctor Lee took the basket and placed it on the ground so all could see. With white cotton gloves on, he lifted up a small, brown clay pot, cracked and chipped from the weight of the tomb roof that had partially sunk in over the casket. The pot was a gift to the dead, placed next to the coffin just before burial. Jin-Soo's hands shook as flashbulbs popped and the whir of television cameras broke the silence.

Jin-Soo nodded. "It is from the Silla era, but why it is here and not at the ancient Silla capital of Kyongju, I cannot say. This will be a wonderful mystery to unravel. For now, let us say we have definitely discovered a royal tomb. Perhaps not that of an emperor, as we had hoped. But whoever is buried here was important, and the finds will be equally important."

A slow roar rose from the crowd as excited reporters gathered around to see the small, unglazed pot.

The mayor stood up. "We will organize a full-scale excavation." Jin-Soo nodded with approval.

Prince Yee and the mayor were photographed with Jin-Soo holding the pot aloft. They were so absorbed in the discovery they did not notice Clover leaving. She couldn't keep up a facade of normalcy much more. And the discovery was for the Koreans to revel in; she wanted to let them enjoy the moment together. She was an outsider, and so exhausted from work and emotional stress that she was dizzy.

The multiple assaults on her passions had taken their toll. A blind unreasonable rage overtook her when she reached her office and found the door ajar—she remembered closing it—and the sounds of someone rummaging through papers.

Furiously she slammed the door open against the wall and stopped, shocked. The last person in the world she expected to see was the senior partner in her firm—David Thompson.

He jumped at her stormy entrance, then said, "Clover!"

"David! I didn't . . . I'm stunned. Why didn't you tell me you were coming?"

David waved an unopened cablegram that he had picked up from Betty's desk. "Don't you read your mail or open your cables?"

Clover sank down in a chair in the reception area, her face streaked with dirt and perspiration, her clothes disheveled. She was totally unprepared for David's arrival.

"Have you been overworking again?" He knelt down in front of her and pushed back her hair. "I had a suspicion you were trying to hold up the whole business alone. And that little note you penned about Devereaux at the bottom of your letter was like a bomb. Since I had other business here I decided to look in on you."

She felt as if David had pulled a plug and drained out her reserve energy.

"Why didn't you just call for help?" he asked quietly.

She was running on pure adrenaline now. After a long pause she said hollowly, "I couldn't, and Betty needed a vacation."

"So you decided you could do it alone. Men call for help when they need it. Women can, too, without losing face."

Clover shook her head. "No, they can't."

David sighed, exasperated. "All of the turmoil and work can be handled by Miss Independence, right? I know more about what's been happening here than you think. So I cabled that I'd arrive today. When you didn't meet me at the airport, I came ahead. I'm staying at the Shilla." He waved the unopened cable in front of her again and tossed it aside.

"Oh, David, I'm so sorry. The temporary secretary didn't come in today and I just started the report on a new project site, and then Doctor Lee dragged me to the opening of the tomb. And God, I'm so tired."

"Whoa," he said, holding his hand up. "One thing at a time. First, tell me about Devereaux. Your letter sounded as if you suspected him of some kind of chicanery."

"It's been in the back of my mind. But I think I might be wrong. He was at the temporary site today getting the trailers positioned. I wanted to help, but he was angry and yelling at everyone. Then Jin-Soo Lee—uh, Doctor Lee—came along and I left to watch him open the tomb. I honestly don't think I could have helped Roarke, but I neglected him, my job, the river-dwellers, everyone, just to look at a damned tomb."

"It just occured to me that it isn't the job or the tomb, but Devereaux, who's undoing you.

"No!"

"Anger can swallow up the hurt, Clover. But it still shows. Are you in love with him?"

"No, I tell you! I'm not! I mean . . ." She looked at David, the man who had hired her and become her mentor. It was David who had urged her to bid for the Yong Dong Pō contract, who guided her career. Now it was kind, patient David who soothed the ruffled feathers of her pride.

"Our relationship never compromised my work," she assured him.

"I know that, young lady. It probably had the opposite effect, if I know you. You just worked harder and scrutinized the plans more closely. But whatever you and Roarke have going has made an emotional wreck out of you."

She nodded her head in agreement. "I have one more thing to do here, David; then I'm going home."

"Dinner later?" he asked.

"Love it. We also have to talk about the contract that Devereaux Enterprises got."

"I'll handle that . . . no, Clover, I'll handle it," he repeated as Clover tried to interrupt him in protest. "The legal aspects of Thompson Associates still belong to me," he said.

Too tired to argue, she acquiesced. David smiled and stood up, groaning aloud as his knees creaked. Clover laughed with him and stood up to see him out of the office.

Alone again, she stared at the wall behind Betty's desk. She hadn't felt so light-headed and tormented, so pulled toward an abyss of fear, love, and unspeakable confusion, since John's death. She loved Roarke. She admitted that now to herself. But she wasn't at all sure what to do about it.

A shudder passed through her. Lifting her head, she saw a looming, dark shadow in the doorway. Roarke!

8

"Why didn't you stay at the trailer site a while ago?" He spoke abruptly, his husky deep voice vibrating with sexuality.

"You were busy. I didn't want to bother you," she answered coolly.

"You ran off so fast. I want to know why."

"I wanted to see the tomb opened. Jin-Soo had come for me. Besides, I could hear you shouting—your language was very explicit." She tilted her face and looked into his eyes.

"That damned tomb again. It means more to you than I or the river-dwellers do."

"I'll decide the priorities in my life. How dare you accuse me of that!" Clover walked smartly into her office and slammed the door behind her, angry with herself for losing her temper.

A quiet chill settled over her office. Clover braced herself for the dreadful scene sure to follow. Roarke would never let her emotional outburst go unchallenged. He finally opened the door, the one she had just slammed in his face, and charged in.

She steadied herself against a wall of her office as Roarke headed straight for her. She stared at him in detached fascination. She had wanted to discuss the tomb with him, to share her excitement, but his recalcitrant attitude had tipped her tired emotions over the edge. She was suddenly very weary of the ups and downs, the overheated ambitions of men, and the politics of love.

He grabbed her wrist, pulled her around the desk, and sat her down hard on one of her own monk's chairs.

With remarkable self-control after his blazing entry into her office, he leaned over her. "I want you to tell me just what your priorities are. I'm sick to death of this tomb business. It appears to me to be the only thing that has meaning in your life."

She gave him her best stony glare. "If what we had in Cheju Dō and Hong Kong hasn't convinced you, nothing will."

"There's a big difference between love and sex," he stated coolly.

Clover was so nonplussed, she just stared at him. Then she started to laugh. "Look who's talking. The innocent Mr. Roarke Devereaux. Did I take unfair advantage of you? Did I seduce you against your will? Poor Roarke. My God, you have a way of turning the truth upside down. You libertine! You should talk. Your exploits are public—oh yes, I've read about them in the paper. But when someone challenges you, you become the innocent bystander. Baloney, Roarke. You're pure baloney!" She was so mad that she felt like crying, but she'd be damned if she would let him see her in tears. It was bad enough not to be able to always control one's temper. But tears she *would* control. Calmly she asked, "What about the contract, Roarke. Did you get it fairly?" This time she knew she had belted him across the old male ego.

"Do you have to ask?" His voice was flat, defeated. She was silent, waiting for him to tell her that she was wrong. Instead, he responded with cold fury. "Clover, you are way out of line." He was silent a moment, then he continued more calmly, "You realize that it isn't this tomb, or Myune, or the contract on trial. It's us." Roarke looked genuinely sad and let go of her wrist and backed away.

"We always get back to that. Us."

"You have to believe in me and I in you. I told you once that I can't live my life with someone who's suspicious of my every move. I need a woman to love, a woman who believes in me. You don't. You let gossip and rumor rule your opinion of others . . . of me."

Clover hesitated, unsure of how to respond to him. He was right about her and she realized how much more they needed of that precious commodity called time. Time to talk, time to explain, and time to heal wounds that neither meant to inflict on the other.

She wanted to know him better, to talk to him and smooth out the misunderstandings, but her exhausted emotions had made her incautious and angry, and it had all come out against the man she was in love with.

"Someday, Clover," Roarke interrupted her thoughts, "you might get to know me. I hope it won't be too late."

"I want to believe you, Roarke. But you seem to continually be testing me. I can't live with that, either."

Roarke's stabbing look softened. "You might try harder." He turned and left, gently closing the door after him. She knew beyond a doubt that Roarke was finished with her—and she couldn't blame him.

Clover had reached a point past exhaustion, when one moves mechanically—without thought and on borrowed energy. She stood up slowly and walked out the door, picked up her purse from the reception room floor where she had dropped it, and left.

Out on the street she hailed a cab. The ride to her apartment was brief and she let the scenery that had always captivated her blur outside the car window. Even the rare appearance of a rickety two-wheeled wooden cart drawn by a yellow ox failed to move her spirit. She let it pass in the same indistinct cloud of hurt and fatigue as she did the rest of Seoul.

After she let herself into her tidy, fashionable apartment, she collapsed on her bed. She fell into a deep dreamless sleep in which a persistent pounding was the only subconscious noise. Footsteps and a voice finally accompanied the pounding. The voice grew louder, but she couldn't make sense of it. Who was it? Why didn't he go away? She felt a hand on her shoulder and someone, she didn't know who, called her name and shook her.

Time and space were irrelevant. When she opened her eyes she momentarily forgot where she was.

"Clover! For God's sake, wake up. Are you ill?"

But Clover thought if she closed her eyes he'd go away. Darkness, blessed darkness, descended over her brain. She felt herself drift away, out of body, over the land, green and peaceful. But the male voice wouldn't let her rest.

"Clover. Wake up. Come on, Clover."

She tried to push him away but she couldn't move her arm. Someone had tied her down. Panic set in. She heard herself cry out but it was all too nebulous—the voice calling her name, the shaking motion, and her arms and legs tied down. She couldn't make her mind work. She couldn't remember who she was or exactly what she was doing. But she wasn't doing anything, was she?

"Clover, wake up."

She opened her eyes again. A face loomed above her, and she finally recognized David Thompson.

"Sit up, Clover." David gently raised her shoulders and plumped a pillow behind her.

"Where am I?" she asked. Her voice seemed more normal to her now as the room came into focus.

"It's all right, Clover. When I arrived for our dinner date you didn't answer your door. Luckily you left it unlocked, so I came in after pounding on it for a while. I found you here—out like a damned light."

Clover shook her head. "How long was I out?"

"I guess about an hour or so. You scared the hell out of me. You're fatigued, that's all."

She squinted, trying hard to understand. David's voice came through the fog lingering in her mind.

"You tried to take on too much. It caught up with you," he said.

"Oh," she replied, utterly bewildered.

"I'll fix your dinner and then you can get back to sleep."

"Let me shower first," she answered. "I feel like I'm covered with grime." Sheer fatigue slowed her down as she padded across the room. David watched her with a tense wariness, as if she might collapse in a dusty heap.

"I'm okay," she said, waving him away. "I'll be out in a minute. Thanks."

Clover welcomed the cold water that beat down on her in the shower. She stood still and turned her face toward the shower head, letting her hair get soaked. She lathered, rinsed, and got out, drying herself off vigorously. Slipping into a terry robe, she turned the hair dryer on high, fluffing her hair into a mass of curls and ringlets.

"Dinner's ready!" David's voice was cheerful, but Clover recognized a worried strain in it.

She had washed away some of the fatigue and was almost, but not quite, her cheerful self. However, with her mind functioning again came the painful memory of her recent quarrel with Roarke. She tried to push the tangled thoughts away. She squared her shoulders and walked out to the kitchen. "Smells good. I didn't know you could cook, too!"

David laughed. "You have a well-stocked fridge for a liberated feminist."

"David!"

"Sit down." He motioned to her dining table that he had set with her good china and silver. He pointed to the matches. "I said I was taking you to dinner. Let's do it right. Light the candles, please."

She struck the match furiously without results, then dropped the matchbook. Leaning over, she felt dizzy, and grabbed the edge of the table. David had been watching and rushed over.

"Here, let me." His face reflected concern as he neatly struck a match and lit the candles.

"I'm all right. Really."

"Yeah. Sure." He trotted back into the kitchen, banged about for a few minutes, then emerged with two plates heaped with food.

"Oh, David, it looks delicious. I was hungrier than I thought."

"Eat," he ordered gently.

Clover was amazed at the succulent cuisine her boss had put together. She realized as they ate in silence how little she really knew about him. He had taken her in after John's death, and an empathy had grown between them because David had also recently lost his spouse. A strong professional friendship had resulted, a friendship that was comfortable to both.

Now she took time to look at him. She studied his face, a face much younger than his fifty-five years, tanned, unlined, and elegantly chiseled. Only his shock of perfectly groomed white hair gave his age away.

Slight and lean, David fit the description of a typical executive—in charge of his life and his company, and always at home wherever he went. After he graduated from Cornell, David had built David Thompson Associates from a one-man, one-secretary planning firm to a multimillion-dollar planning and engineering conglomerate with contracts all over the globe.

Clover was flattered that her minuscule contract in Yong Dong Pō had attracted his attention. But that's why David was successful—he never let a single small problem or minor contract go unnoticed by him personally.

"Thinking too hard has always been your downfall. The wheels are spinning, Clover. Care to tell me about Devereaux?"

"I was thinking about you. This is the first time something personal has entered our lives together. I just realized that I know very little about David Thompson the man. Like, where did you learn to cook this way?"

"Cooking is a hobby. I've even taught a night course in cooking for bachelors." David's eyes twinkled at the fun of revealing a part of himself no one in the firm knew, except Clover now.

"Amazing," she whispered. "I won't tell."

David grinned. "Now, about Devereaux."

He wouldn't let it go no matter how cleverly she tried to change the subject, so she drew a deep breath. "I've suspected from the first that something wasn't right about the engineering phase of the contract. But I let my personal feelings . . ." She stopped and looked up from her half-eaten dinner to assess David's reaction. Seeing none, she continued. "I let my considerable personal feelings interfere with my judgement. I ignored the niggling thought that said something was wrong. We seem to disagree alot on everything. The tomb discovery capped our differences. He's against it, I'm for it. And so forth. We just had another argument—it was my fault this time and I brought up what has been bothering me all along. The contract."

David said, "After I left you this afternoon, I called on an old friend, who shall remain anonymous, and asked him about it. This man is very well-placed in the government and knows every damned thing going on. Seems the whole bid process was aboveboard. He did get the contract fair and square."

Clover's heart flipped over and stuck in her throat. "You're sure?"

"Yes. I trust this man's word as if he were my brother. I saved his life during the war and we've been as close as kin since. I think you certainly had reason to suspect, but you were wrong."

David's bluntness stunned her. "After questioning him about whether or not he got the contract fairly, he'll never forgive me. I really blew it, didn't I?"

"Did you?"

"Wouldn't you say I did?" Clover asked.

"If someone just about accused me of dishonesty, I'd be pounding mad. However, I wouldn't have been so careless as to let the appearance of wrongdoing shine quite so bright. In his innocence, he was a little naive."

"That doesn't help me," she added.

"Eat," he said. "Things will work out. He'd be a fool to let you go."

Clover ate the rest of her dinner ravenously, gulping the wine to drown out the confusion she felt. She successfully suppressed waves of muted hysteria inside and kept her exterior facade poised and calm.

But a sharp knock at the door made her jump and drop her fork.

"I'll get it." David stood up, threw his napkin on the table, and walked over to the door, and opened it. Roarke charged in. A brief silence engulfed them, during which they all stared at each other in suspended animation.

"Well," Roarke said, "isn't this cozy!" He glared at Clover, sitting in her bathrobe at the candlelit table.

Clover, whose mind at the moment was just about ten

seconds behind everyone else's, didn't understand his reaction. She frowned, puzzled.

David, looking confident and smug as usual, leaned against the open door and waited.

"Uh, Roarke, this is David Thompson. David, this is Roarke Devereaux."

David held his hand out, but Roarke ignored him, instead stalking into the room further to confront Clover. His face reflected angrily aroused passions as he towered over the table. "You have one hell of a nerve accusing me of being a—how did you put it? A libertine? Just what is it called when you walk in on the woman who's supposed to love you and find her sitting in her bathrobe with another man?" he shouted at her.

"Roarke, David's my boss."

"He's a man and I don't give a damn what his title is. You're in your bathrobe!"

"I can explain . . ."

"I bet you'd come up with a doozy, too."

"Just a minute, Devereaux." David had apparently had enough. He walked over and put his hand on Roarke's shoulder—the wrong gesture to make toward a jealous man.

Roarke turned and took a swing at David, who ducked neatly out of the way.

Clover watched, appalled.

"And you. What're you doing in Clover's apartment?" Roarke's voice had risen a few more decibels.

"Lower your voice, Devereaux. The lady has a reputation to maintain."

"Then she shouldn't be entertaining men in her bathrobe," Roarke said, balling his fists up but keeping them at his side.

David shut the front door. "Look, let's talk." He gestured to a chair at the table.

Roarke didn't budge, his face turned a deep purple and the veins flared out at his temples. He turned back to Clover.

"I came over to try and settle our differences. But, since you're busy—"

"Sit down, Devereaux," David ordered.

"No, thank you."

"Don't be an ass. You walk out now and someone else will step into your place. You'll lose her for good."

Roarke gaped at David. He'd been challenged but seemed unsure what to do about the situation.

"You?" Roarke roared. "She's mine."

Clover stared at Roarke and David, who had suddenly taken on the appearance and stance of two little boys quarreling over their marbles. As if she wasn't there, they kept up the barrage of verbal warfare.

"I think, Devereaux, she's not anyone's property. If you had taken the time to know her, you'd realize what a gem she is—an independent, thinking woman with a strong will and a mind of her own." David's voice had grown loud, and he attempted to lower it. "So don't play games with her."

"Who's playing games? It looks like a few games have been played here tonight."

This time David lost his head and smacked Roarke in the nose. Before either could react they both turned and started toward Clover, who had burst into hysterical laughter. From her red face and shaking hands, it was clear she was close to total collapse.

"It seems we're both bloody fools, Devereaux," David said in a calm voice. "She was sick when I arrived earlier. That's why she's in her bathrobe. She's exhausted. Help me get her back to bed."

"My God, what've we done to her?" she heard Roarke say as they helped her to her room. She felt dizzy, still laughing, angry that she was no longer in control. The voices quickly dimmed and she felt her mind and body slip away in the secure comfort of her bed.

It was a strange and exciting journey that perforce would end when the fatigue and pain of the last few weeks were blissfully slept away. The last bit of consciousness she was aware of was a hand slipping into hers, and the feeling lingered deep into her dreams.

Her dream's journey took her to a pine forest alive with the scent of trees and fresh air, a place where hurt, bitterness, and the tensions in her life were swept away on fragrant breezes.

Roarke was there, too. She saw him standing near a tall pine tree, arms akimbo, wearing a smile for her alone. He was a very long way off and she would have to cross the forest to get to him. His masculine, pantherlike grace beckoned her and she ran toward him. Branches of bushes and trees, of low-lying shrubs, and of her own doubts flung themselves in her way, but she fought to reach him. He stood quietly, watching her. By his stance she knew he would not help her. She had questioned his honesty. So now she would have to prove that she did not mean what she had said. She would have to fight to get him back.

She fell. The sun was going down behind her, the forest becoming dark and sinister. Roarke was outlined in a brilliant fire of orange, with the deep green of the trees behind and around him.

"I hope you won't reach me too late, Clover. Too late!" His voice boomed out at her, reaching a crescendo as the breezes began to whip up the pine boughs around her.

"Roarke, help me!" she called out, struggling to regain her footing.

"No! When you reach me on your own, then I'll know you love me. But I can't help you anymore," he answered.

"Please, Roarke!" she called again.

He didn't answer her but stood still, waiting. All she saw was Roarke and she wanted to get to him. The wind was strong now and she had to peer into the distance at a fast-fading figure of the man she loved and could not reach. How could this be happening to her? If only she could find a path, then it would be easy.

Roarke seemed to be laughing at her. The implication was clear: This was a test! That's why she was having so much difficulty. Well, I'll show him. I'll get there. Clover ran, frightened but also elated that she could make amends for her rash accusations.

Before she realized it, a hand reached out for her. She had reached him, finally. She wanted to hold him, never to let him go again. He pulled her down to the soft warm forest floor, under the pine tree he had been standing next to.

Gently his long, slender hands caressed her as he began a slow, meticulous pilgrimage of seduction.

The barriers fell away as she lay back on the scented pine floor listening subconsciously to the whispering wind above. His hand cupped her chin.

"Love me," he commanded. She looked up at him. His chest heaved in deep breaths as she touched the buttons on his shirt. One by one, she opened them, running her fingers through his hair, touching the hollow of his throat, gently moving over his nipples that hardened at her merest caress. She moved her hands lower, following the line of his hair as it disappeared beneath his belt. Her fingers, eager and demanding, fumbled with his trousers as his soft laugh echoed above her.

"Need help again?" he asked. His eyes crinkled with amusement.

She couldn't answer. She was frantic to see him naked above her and she pulled not too gently at his belt. His hand reached over and snapped the belt open for her and in one quick movement she watched with erotic fascination as he threw off his shirt and trousers.

The flawless, masculine, tanned body that had always sent her blood boiling through her veins dropped down beside her and his hands reached out to undress her. Hard, throbbing sensations coursed through her as she felt him pull at her blouse and skirt. His hands and fingers reached for her breasts, caressing them gently. One hand slid down to her thighs and began a circling motion that drove her to speechless ecstasy.

He pulled her to him and tightened his hold on her, pressing her against him. His lips seared her as he made his maddening way from her forehead, down her nose to her lips. His mouth plunged down on hers, and his tongue explored her, pressing the white hot desires deeper into her when she suddenly, and without hindrance, pulled him over her and wrapped her legs around his waist, thrusting herself against him until he pulled his mouth away and uttered a groan that echoed on the winds throughout the forest. The trees picked the sound up and she heard the insistent voices around her, groaning and sighing along with Roarke.

She was out of control as she moved against him harder and deeper until Roarke was totally within her, part of her, more of her than any man had ever been. She twisted erotically against him, eliciting from him shuddering breaths and loud moans. He, too, had forgotten who was the seducer and who was the seduced. She had reached him over miles of forest and now she would take from him every ounce of his sexual energy, pulling it into her own body.

"Clover, don't ever leave me. I need you. You excite me more than any woman or anything in my life." His voice was hoarse. "I can't live without you. I can't go on without you next to me, loving me. Please, stay here." Roarke called out to her as she unleashed her frantic needs. All she knew now was that Roarke was there for her to love as she wished. They were hidden from the world, under a tree in a forest so far from reality that only the two of them knew where it was.

His hands held her buttocks tight, pressing her against him, keeping her from pulling away. But she had no desire to pull from him. All that counted was to have Roarke a part of her, all of her.

Her mouth accepted his eager kisses, her body his warm, hard need of her. They became as one, twisting and touching in a stormy fire born of desperate need that did not seem to abate but grow as desire fed desire.

When the fire did pass, it stopped abruptly. They pulled apart and lay on their sides, watching each other. The wind ceased, the tree branches quieted, the birds chirped softly. Silence engulfed them and she slept, long and deep, sated as only she could be with Roarke.

It took several minutes to comprehend where she was, but the persistent bird finally woke her. Instead of a forest nest under a pine tree, she was back in her own bedroom. The sun was trying to get through her curtains, and she could smell fresh-brewed coffee. Her body, rather than being relaxed from loving, was stiff and sore. She raised her head and shook it. Obviously she wasn't in the middle of a forest after a night with Roarke. Disappointment wafted over her momentarily, but she was regaining her reason and sensibilities and was glad to find herself in her own bed.

She sat up and moved her head in deep circles to release the tension in her neck. Flinging the covers aside, she got up and wobbled into her bathroom. She was still in her terry robe but realized that she was stark naked under it. She frowned in the mirror and tried to remember what had happened the night before. David had fixed her dinner and then he and someone else had put her to bed, she thought. Roarke? Did I dream it all? Roarke did not visit her last night. Or did he?

Damn, she muttered, and wondered where her head was. What, she mused, *did* happen last night? She splashed her face with water and pulled another robe from her closet and put it on. The coffee fragrance was so enticing that she walked toward the door that opened onto the dining room.

When she opened it and looked out, a little apprehensive, Roarke was standing there, grinning.

"Good afternoon, sleepyhead," he said.

"What're you doing here?"

"No 'Hello Roarke, and how are you'? And I'm making breakfast or lunch, whatever, for you. Come on out; I won't bite, promise."

Clover walked out to her dining room and sat down at the table. Her best china and remnants of last night's dinner candles were still in place.

"How long did I sleep?" she asked.

"About fourteen hours."

"Where's David?"

"He went back to his hotel."

"You stayed? All night?"

"Uh-huh."

Roarke brought her coffee and waffles. She picked at them, then looked at Roarke, who had sat at the table opposite her.

"I stayed with you to make sure if you needed someone I'd be here," he announced, still grinning.

Clover's eyes widened. "Did we spend the whole night here?"

"Of course. Where else?"

"In a forest?"

Roarke threw his head back and laughed. "A forest?"

"A pine forest. You were standing next to a tree."

"Not me." He smiled.

"Did we make love?"

"Not last night, sweetheart. I expect more response

than an unconscious woman is capable of giving. Why? Is that why you were so restless?"

Clover blushed furiously.

"You dreamed it," he said. "Hope it was good."

"Damn you, Roarke. I'm trying to put the last twenty-four hours together, and you make fun of me."

"I'm not making fun of you. After David and I put you back to bed, he explained that you were exhausted and that's why I found you in your bathrobe with him. We had a long talk about you, and I told him why I was angry about your being with another man." Roarke shrugged. "He seemed to accept it. Anyway, I cleaned up the dishes, sort of, and slept with you for about eight hours. You really thrashed around for a while, then stopped and slept sound the rest of the night and into today."

"Roarke . . ." She sat down and took a deep breath. "I was out of line yesterday. Then you came in here demanding to know what I'm doing with David—oh yes, I remember a little of what happened last evening. You were downright nasty. In fact, I think you and David acted like two little children."

Roarke snorted. "I guess we did. He poked me in the nose."

"David?"

Roarke nodded.

Clover couldn't picture David getting physical during an argument, and she smiled. "Good for him. Maybe someone had to."

"Thanks," Roarke said, stabbing a piece of waffle with his fork.

"Love isn't a one-way street, Roarke. You have to give as much as I do. You can't continually expect me to agree with you about everything. I can't live with that."

"Okay, damn it. Have your . . . tomb. Who the hell cares about it?"

"David told me how wrong I was about the contract."

Clover looked at Roarke. "How can I possibly make up for thinking you may have cheated?"

"Try to learn to trust people."

"I will. But I was deeply hurt when you accused me of not caring. I care, Roarke. About the river-dwellers, you, Myune."

"Hey, I know, Clover. We both said things we didn't mean yesterday."

"I'd made up my mind to tell you I love you, Roarke. I couldn't keep it inside anymore. I was scared when I got to the site. You were busy—angry—but we've been over this."

Roarke stopped eating and put his fork down. "Whatever happened to the woman who met all challenges? The one who never ran away?"

"Jin-Soo came to get me. They were about to open the burial area, so I left with him. They did find an unglazed pot. You've heard, I'm sure."

Roarke said, "Like I said, they think more about their pots and artifacts than about living, feeling people."

Clover despaired. This seemed like the insurmountable barrier that continually came between them.

"I don't want to argue about that now," she answered tartly.

"Storm clouds are gathering in your eyes, my love. How can we think about living our lives together if there's even one small subject we can't discuss? It won't work."

"You're so damned unreasonable about it," she cried out. "It isn't even your business to judge these people's culture but you make a habit out of it."

Roarke sighed and said, "Somewhere along the way you'll find a man who agrees with you one hundred percent. On everything. That way you won't have to alter your opinions one little bit. The thought of you in the arms of another man . . . Do you really think of me as insensitive? Maybe if you had taken the time to know me, you'd know I hurt, I feel, I love, and I can get just as scared as you when the trap closes in on me. I question, too. Is it right? Can I make her happy? Will I be a good husband? Marriage, you say? You *bet* I think about it. Women aren't the only ones who want to stop the merry-go-round and live a normal life. But damn it all, I need the same things you do. Love. Trust. Having interests in common. The whole ball of wax."

"Don't go, Roarke," she pleaded.

"Why should I stay? What do we have except the shared joy of loving now and then? I'm selfish, Clover. I want it all."

She sank back into her chair. "Then go, Roarke, if you think we can't make it because we dare to disagree on something. I'm not a perfect woman, I don't pretend to be, but I love you. Remember that."

Roarke's hand was on the doorknob, but he did not open the door to leave. "There was so much I wanted to . . . to say to you."

A furious pounding on the door startled them both. Roarke opened the door, and Myune came bursting in. "Clover, Clover." He ran over to her and threw himself into her lap. "She's going to send me away, Clover. Don't let her, please," he sobbed into her shoulder.

"Shhh, Myune," she comforted the little boy. "Tell me what you mean. Who's going to send you away?"

Roarke closed the door and walked over to Clover, placing his hand on Myune's head.

"Mrs. Kaeng is sending me to some uncle on a farm. I'll have to work there, and I won't go to school anymore," he wailed.

"I thought Mrs. Kaeng told me she was your only living relative? Who is this farmer?"

"He's in a place called Hamyang."

Roarke said, "It's a valley near the Sobaek Mountains, south of here."

"A long way away," sobbed Myune.

"When did she say you're going?"

"Tomorrow, Clover. He's coming for me tomorrow."

"If they're his legitimate relatives, there's not a damn thing we can do," Roarke whispered.

"I'll move heaven and earth to keep Myune here," she said. "Will you help us, Roarke?"

"Yes, of course. I'll help. We'll do something."

Clover felt her insides twist. A depressing weight pushed down on her as if a piece of her life was falling away. Roarke and Myune were her life, as much as she tried to deny it, and now she would have to fight for them both.

9

Interfering with a child's family is touchy," Roarke said, sitting down in a chair next to Clover and Myune.

"I wonder," Clover mused, "if Mrs. Kaeng ever had proof of her relationship to Myune? How do we find that out?"

"First things first, Clover. If that farmer is coming for Myune tomorrow, we'll have to stop him now. I have a banker friend named Kim. I'll call to see what he suggests."

"Kim? The Bank of Seoul?" Clover shuddered. "Please, Roarke, call on the devil himself if it will help."

Roarke pointedly ignored Clover's remark as he picked up the phone and dialed. After a few moments he said, "Mr. Kim, please. Roarke Devereaux. It's urgent." Roarke gave Clover and a sniffling Myune an encouraging smile.

"Yes, Kyu, thanks for coming to the phone. I need your advice. Mrs. McBain and I have taken a small boy named

Myune under our, uh, protection. He lives with an old woman who has some vague claim on him. A problem just came up. This woman is sending Myune to work with a farmer in Hamyang tomorrow. Is there any way to get an order to stop his move until we satisfy ourselves about the legitimacy of their claim on the boy?"

Roarke frowned deeply as he listened. "I see. Will anyone do? A Korean. I understand. Good . . . Who? Is he related to the industrialist? He is? What good luck! Thank you, I will."

Clover was ready to climb into the telephone when Roarke hung up. "Well?" She bubbled over with anticipation.

"It pays to be nice to everyone!" he roared.

"Other than the obvious reasons, tell me why?"

"The Minister of Health and Social Affairs is the brother of none other than Mr. Hwang—the man we hunted with on Cheju Dō!"

Clover let out a whoop and hugged a bewildered Myune.

"Now, listen up, Clover," Roarke said. "We need a Korean to temporarily sponsor Myune until Mrs. Kaeng and the farmer can prove their claim to be his relatives." He looked hard at her. "Who are you going to ask?"

Clover covered her mouth with her hand and frowned. "Prince Yee. He did offer to help—if we needed it."

Roarke handed the phone to Clover. "Dial."

Clover hesitated, then dialed and waited.

"Hello? This is Clover McBain. May I speak to His Highness, please?" She gave Roarke a furtive look and took a deep breath.

"Prince Yee? I need to ask a very big favor of you. It's for Myune. The woman he lives with wants to send him away to a farmer in Hamyang. She says the man is an 'uncle.' We, uh, Roarke and I will ask for a temporary restraint of the boy's move until Mrs. Kaeng can prove her relationship. But—" She stopped, then brightened.

"Yes! Would you? Oh, thank you so much! We'll bring Myune over immediately then go to the Ministry of Health and Social Affairs after. Good-bye."

Clover turned to Roarke. "He offered right away." She pushed Myune's hair back. "Do you understand what we're doing, sweetheart?" she asked the boy.

Myune shook his head.

"We are going to stop Mrs. Kaeng from sending you to Hamyang—at least for a while. But a Korean must be willing to sponsor you while the inquiry into your relationship with Mrs. Kaeng is investigated. Prince Yee has offered to take you into his home during this time. We'll go over there right now."

"Prince Yee? Really?" Myune's eyes widened and he wiped the tears from his face with his sleeve. "Boy," he said solemnly.

By the time they reached the Changdok Palace, at the foot of one of Seoul's many hills, Myune was bursting with anticipation. For the most part their conversation during the ride had been stilted. Roarke and Clover had thrown each other knowing glances over Myune's head. In the end, if Mrs. Kaeng could prove she was Myune's relative, and if the farmer also had a legitimate claim as well, Clover would lose the boy. The law was strict, and all the friends in high places couldn't help.

The thrill of entering the Changdok Palace was as intense for Clover today as it had been the first time she was there and the dozen or so times since. They were led by a servant through the dark wood-paneled entryway and into the prince's private garden. The prince was sitting on a stone bench looking at a brick wall two hundred feet long.

"It symbolizes the continuity of the Yee Dynasty," he said without formality. "There were forty-nine Yee Dynasty kings and queens. I am the last."

Roarke, Clover, and Myune stood quietly, drinking in the exquisite garden.

"Four seasons live in harmony here," the prince continued. "For winter, the evergreen; for spring, the azalea and the blossoming cherry; for summer, water lilies; and for fall, the persimmon." He stopped but did not look at them.

"Do you know the *Song of Five Friends?*" he asked.

It was not appropriate to answer, but Myune nodded that he knew. The prince smiled and held his hand out to the boy.

"Tell me, Myune."

Myune walked over to the prince, took a deep breath, and concentrated on the brick wall.

> *"How many friends have I? Count them:"*
> Myune hesitated.
> *"Water and stone, pine and bamboo—*
> *The rising moon on the east mountain,*
> *Welcome, it too is my friend."*

He looked at the prince for approval. The prince smiled, nodded, and finished the stanza for him:

> *"What need is there, I say,*
> *To have more friends than five?"*

"How beautiful," Clover whispered.

"Let us pray five friends will be enough." The prince looked sadly at Clover and Roarke, who stood apart from them, holding hands. They felt alien—not part of the past or the future as were the prince and Myune—but of the present.

Roarke squeezed Clover's hand and whispered, "We'll win this one, Clover. Have faith in our five friends."

Roarke and Clover spent the remainder of the day trudging from one friend to another. A quick visit to their hunting companion, Mr. Hwang, paid off in a well-placed call to his brother, the Minister of Health and Social Affairs, where the slowly-grinding wheels speeded up considerably. Papers were signed, issued, and presumably delivered to Mrs. Kaeng and the appropriate underlings who would keep the wheels churning in Myune's favor.

Evening fell hard on Seoul. The brilliant red sky, the suffocating humidity of midsummer, and a lingering exhaustion that Clover couldn't shake, pressed down on her. Roarke had taken her to his home, where Mrs. Gee had prepared dinner. After the meal, Clover sat on a wood chair in front of the *koy* pond, with her feet propped up on a rock. Roarke handed her a V.O. and Seven, mostly Seven, she realized, and sat down on the edge of the pond, facing her.

"Everything will be okay, Clover," he said, his voice soft and tender.

"Not if Mrs. Kaeng can prove her claim," she answered.

"Even if she does, we might still keep Myune in Seoul. Stop and think for a minute. Mrs. Kaeng gets about six thousand won a month from the government for Myune. Why would she be willing to give that up?"

Clover sat deathly still, staring at the brightly colored fish playing in the water. She felt a repulsion stir in her, and gave Roarke a shocked look.

"No!" she said, more to convince herself than to convince Roarke.

"Why else?" Roarke shot back. "The farmer is paying her for Myune."

"She's selling him."

"You bet. If we can prove that, the government will take Myune away from her so fast she won't know what happened. And frankly, it wouldn't be difficult to prove. Someone as poor as Mrs. Kaeng won't be able to explain a sudden windfall."

"How *could* she?" Clover spit out.

"Mrs. Kaeng is poor, probably among the poorest in Korea. Who are we to pass judgment? Don't misunderstand. I'm as repulsed at the idea as you are. But it doesn't make her poverty any easier to bear. It's survival, as far as she's concerned."

Clover let tears slide down her cheeks without bothering to wipe them away. She felt as if Myune was her own child—a bright, eager boy, and a joy to be around. The thought of losing him, of someone selling him as if he were a piece of merchandise, made her sick. But she was an American in a country whose values, culture and history made her an alien. The obstacles she would have to hurdle for the boy seemed insurmountable at this moment.

Roarke reached out to her. "Clover. Let's talk about us."

"Us." She said the word but felt the reality was unobtainable.

"Yes, my love. Us. You've been through a lot, all of it alone. Do you want to be alone forever? I don't."

"But we disagree on so much," she answered.

"Do we? Superficial things. I don't really believe it's the tomb excavation or this male-versus-female thing we seem to have gotten involved in that's keeping us apart. You're using it as an excuse. Tell me about John. You never talk about him. I think that's your problem." He smiled at her over the rim of his glass. "Tell me about it, love. Please?"

What could she say now? The tenderness and concern in his voice crumbled her defenses. The ghost haunting her all these years *was* John. His vile accusations, his flaming temper, his macho superiority had reduced her to the kind of woman she had always reviled: a wimp. After his death and her miscarriage, it took her years to push the wimp aside and let the real Clover McBain emerge—a confident, maybe overconfident woman, who needed no man to boost her self-esteem. She had also adopted a "men-be-damned" attitude and carried it around like an Olympic runner's fiery torch.

Roarke's foot reached out and jiggled her leg. His smile was mischievous and loving.

She stirred, restless under his persistent scrutiny. How wrong she had been about him. Her heart had been right all along but her calculating mind had taken over after their initial encounter, allowing only brief moments of truth to interfere with her indecisiveness. The battles between mind and heart had almost destroyed her and any chance of happiness with him.

Right now she had to make a choice, knowing instinctively it was the last opportunity to make the right one. Clover hesitated, then spoke. "Yes. It's been John. We were married only six months, but in that time he tried to reduce me to a totally dependent woman—you know, the kind who sits all day on the fender of his car while he tinkers with the engine, the kind who obeys instantly out of fear—I hated myself for it. I guess I went too far the other way after his death. But the pendulum has swung back toward the middle now."

"Good. Because I dislike the kind of woman you described. I want the real Clover S. McBain." Roarke gave her a bright, warm, lingering smile.

"Oh, Roarke." She set her glass down and threw herself into his arms.

He ran his fingers through her silky hair. "Cry, love. Let it all out."

She wrapped her arms around his neck. The comfort of being secure in his arms, the need to be there, crying, gave her the vitality that she had lacked for months.

Suddenly Roarke's voice cracked with emotion. "Do you know the precise moment when I knew I loved you and would marry you?" he asked.

"Marry?"

"That's right," he whispered. "Roarke Devereaux, who let no woman into his life, made a deliberate decision to marry someone he hardly knew. But something was there between us, underlying all the bickering, the uncertainties. It was there, Clover, long before either of us would admit it and it was damnably strong."

"Well? When?" She pulled her face away to get a better look at him.

"That Saturday morning we went on a picnic with Myune. You were sitting at your desk writing a letter, a deep frown of concentration on your beautiful face. I watched you for a full five minutes and suddenly told myself that one day I'd have you, all of you. That's what I meant on Cheju Dō when I said I shouldn't have let you seduce me that day. Sitting at your desk you were seduction in its purest form. And, by the way, you snap a mean towel. I still have a welt on my rear end."

Clover laughed. "I was writing to David about you that day."

"Aha! The sinister Roarke Devereaux!"

"Little did I know," she said, running her fingers over his face, tracing each line and crevice. "I like your face," she whispered. "And, I'm sorry about your rear end."

"Will you marry me?" He chuckled softly with her. "Clover S. McBain?"

This time she did not hesitate. "Yes." She buried her face in his neck.

The sun dipped below the horizon, casting long, lingering shadows across the courtyard. Clover held tight to Roarke, bursting with a joy she had never known. A quiet settled over them and she could hear Roarke's heart beat wildly, a rhythmic sound reminding her of the underlying passions that had finally captured her body and soul.

Roarke gently picked her up and carried her to his bedroom. Mrs. Gee was nowhere around, but the bed was turned down with a scented gardenia on the pillows. The lighting was soft and gentle; tinkling music drifted in from somewhere.

Roarke laid her on the bed and began removing her clothing one piece at a time. He stopped to admire her body, to caress her skin, and to kiss each newly exposed part of her. She luxuriated in the feeling of complete happiness, fulfillment, and unabashed desire. When Roarke finished removing the last impediment to his own seductive goal, he quickly threw his clothes off and lay down next to her.

"Just to seal the bargain," he mumbled as he kissed her from her neck to her toes. When he nipped her toe playfully, she was reminded of his complaint about the welt on his bottom.

"Roarke, let me see that awful welt I gave you," she asked, half frightened that she had wounded him in anger.

Roarke rolled over and she gasped. The remnant of an angry welt lay diagonally across his buttocks, and she realized that it was her fury that had landed the towel with such lethal accuracy. She touched it gently, then withdrew her hand.

"I'm so sorry. I was terribly angry with you."

He laughed and grabbed her. "By God, it hurt, too."

Then he wrestled her onto her back and growled in her ear. They both stopped suddenly, looking deep into each other's eyes. Without further hesitation, Roarke loved her harder than he ever had before and she responded with a vigor she had not felt in years.

"So, you finally came to your senses." David grinned as he relaxed in the monk's chair in front of her desk.

"If saying 'yes' to Roarke is what coming to my senses means. Can you imagine me married?"

"Certainly, I can. You're much too beautiful and sweet to live a lonely life."

"Thank you for understanding, David. I needed your approval."

"Why, for heaven's sake?"

"Because I like and admire you, and because you're David."

"The real issue here is the new site you've chosen." David blushed and changed the subject. "How's the report going?"

"I finished it." She handed a thick sheaf of papers to him.

"I'll read it tonight, make some comments, and then head back for home. It looks like you have it all under control here."

"Except for Myune," she said sadly. "It's going to take the government forever to make up its mind about him."

"Don't put too much hope on the issue being resolved to your satisfaction. Korea is funny about male children. Even if Mrs. Kaeng isn't a relative, they might not let you and Roarke adopt him."

"Who said anything about adoption?" she asked angrily.

"Don't play innocent with me, young lady. That's precisely what you have in mind."

"Roarke and I have not discussed it," she said imperiously. Her voice softened again. "Right now we want what's best for Myune."

"Just remember that he's a boy and boys are a precious commodity here. A girl wouldn't be a problem. A boy's another story."

"If the time ever comes when Roarke and I think about adopting Myune, we'll do what we have to do to get him."

David shook his head and tucked the report under his arm. "See you tomorrow," he said, and stood up to leave, then hesitated. "I hated to rain on your parade, sweetheart. But someone has to keep reality in front of you. You do tend to drift off into a dreamworld from time to time. Myune might be off limits to you."

"Oh, David. Things are back to normal again. Myune delivers his papers, goes to school, then comes in afterwards to talk and laugh. Everyday it becomes harder to keep up a facade that it will all come out right. Please, don't spoil it for us. Believe it or not, I do know what obstacles are there."

"Clover, Clover. If I could make it happen, I'd do whatever I can. But this is one area that you could lose badly."

Clover shook her head. "No. It will be all right. I know it."

But Clover wasn't sure. After David left she felt a chill in the office. Life was too normal. A new site had been picked, a report written, the advisory committee eager to make a recommendation to the mayor, who was equally eager to show the world that he and his administration did care about the river-dwellers.

And Roarke had finished moving trailers onto the temporary land as he, the Reverend Cho, and a flock of well-meaning volunteers helped the river people move bag, tent, and baggage into a totally alien environment, assuring them it was temporary. The river had risen and flooded them out again; what was left of their meager belongings were put into wooden carts, and hauled up to the trailers. Clover felt sad that a people whose lives revolved around the water were now housed on high ground in modern mobile homes, as sterile and organized as an institution.

But the real energy and excitement remained at the tomb opening. Jin-Soo Lee had made monumental strides toward unearthing the main tomb chamber and was daily pulling more and more earthen jars, bits and pieces of gold jewelry, and jade artifacts out of the hole.

She had been so busy these past weeks with Myune's problem and the report she had to prepare for the advisory committee that she had neglected to keep a curious eye on the excavation. As if by mental telepathy the phone rang. It was Jin-Soo.

"Clover? Why don't you take a break and come to the

tomb? We are at the first casket. Wonderful things are inside and we are going to pull them out. Wear some old clothes and go down into the hole with me."

Clover eagerly agreed. She hurried to her apartment and was changing into her jeans when Roarke called her on the phone.

"Betty told me you went home to change clothes. What're you up to?"

"Oh, Roarke. Jin-Soo called me. They're ready to start bringing the really good artifacts out of the hole. He's invited me to go down with him."

"No," Roarke said quietly.

"No, what?" she asked puzzled.

"I don't want you going down in there. The soil is too unstable. It's dangerous."

"They've shored it up, Roarke. It's perfectly safe."

"No, damn it."

"What's the real reason you don't want me to go?"

"Let's not get into that argument again."

"Then tell me why you don't want me to go down."

Roarke took a deep breath that Clover could hear clearly over the phone. "It isn't safe." His voice sounded pouty and Clover felt her temper flare in response.

"I wonder if that's the real reason." Her voice dripped with deliberate sarcasm—but she was immediately sorry.

Before she could apologize, Roarke shot back, "Isn't my 'no' enough? When in hell are you going to trust me?"

"This has nothing to do with trust. I want to see what's happening! You told me you don't like to be ordered around. Neither do I like to be dictated to. If you think the site is unsafe, why don't you go out there and tell them how to make it safe?"

"Jin-Soo's supposed to be an engineer," Roarke answered. "He won't truck interference."

"But he's never practiced engineering. He's been an archaeologist for as long as I know."

"I give up on you, love. All right, I'll meet you out there."

"Great!" she said cheerfully.

"But only to satisfy myself that it's safe."

Clover hung up and finished dressing. She hailed a cab and urged the driver to hurry to the tomb site.

When she finally found Jin-Soo it amused her to see him both professorial and boyish at the same time, and she grinned inwardly. He was so wrapped up in the excavation that he only nodded when she joined him in the cavernous hole that led to the inner tomb at an oblique angle from the top.

The excitement that Howard Carter must have felt when he peered into King Tut's tomb rippled through her and she knew the dozen or so men who kneeled down around the badly deteriorated casket of the deceased royal were fidgeting with suppressed emotions. Gently they began to lift broken pieces of the ancient lacquered wood away. Through the sticky mud and grime of many centuries came the unmistakable glitter of gold.

Lying in perfect serenity, the corpse, all but gone, could be distinguished by the position of the crown, necklaces, bracelets, garter, and leg and ankle jewelry that were intact, looking as if they were put there a few days ago. Jade and intricate gold were woven into exquisite ornaments. Next to the body were precious pottery jars still filled with unguents, and pots and vases whose colors were as brilliant as the day they were made, even though the dirt and mud covered much of them. Other artifacts could be seen partially sticking up through the bottom of the casket and around the burial area.

As they cleared the mud away, picked the jewelry up, and laid it on carefully prepared trays, pieces of the dirt roof rained down on them. Jin-Soo looked up, a worried expression on his face. The same expression was etched on Roarke's face as he bent over behind them.

"Roarke," Clover said, surprised, "I'm glad you're here. Look at this." She pointed to the casket.

"Splendid," he said sarcastically.

"But," Jin-Soo said, "something is wrong, is it not?"

"I came down to tell you that although your shoring and beams are more than adequate, you have a section of unstable soil that needs compacting. I suggest you all leave this area now while the crews bring in equipment to compact the soil."

"I think you may be right, Roarke," Jin-Soo said. "We just had a small warning from above."

Clover squeezed out of the hole, followed by Jin-Soo, the student workers, and finally Roarke. At the top, Roarke pointed out the unstable area to Jin-Soo, who agreed that within the last several hours the soil had sunken down. He assured the workers it would be a matter of an hour or so to fix the area so it would be safe to continue working in the hole.

Jin-Soo talked to Roarke while Clover and the crowd that had gathered to see the gold jewelry gawked like children in a candy store.

"Thank you for helping me with the shoring. I know you have a great deal of knowledge about the soils here. Is there any other spot we should keep an eye on?" Jin-Soo smiled at Roarke, but Clover could see the strain in his face.

Roarke said, "Yeah. Over by that old beam I think you might have problems. Frankly, I would have an engineering student checking the footing constantly. You never know when a sudden shift might occur, but there's always enough advanced warning if someone is keeping vigil."

"That is a very good idea. I will call for volunteers immediately."

Clover watched Roarke grin spontaneously at Jin-Soo, whose volunteer program was legend. She walked over to Roarke. "Didn't you feel something down in that hole?"

"Chilly. You should dress warmer if you're going to turn into a mole."

"Oh, Roarke. We've just opened a very important tomb, and you were there. You must have had some reaction other than it was chilly."

Roarke grinned. "You want me to say I was thrilled? Okay. It was interesting. The old boy looked a little sticky but his outfit was nice."

Roarke's humorous sarcasm left Clover shaking her head.

"As soon as they clean everything, Prince Yee will display it for the public in that large room in the palace. He's as excited as Jin-Soo," Clover told Roarke.

"Prince Yee is a generous man. Taking Myune without question, for example. Not many men in his position would be so helpful."

"Speaking of Myune, Roarke. Has anyone heard whether Mrs. Kaeng has responded to the government's inquiry?"

"No. But I suggest we go over to the Ministry and ask. It's been too damned long, for me."

"Let me go back to the apartment and change," she said.

"Why? You look fine."

"I'm all dirty."

"Hey, I think you look sexy."

"But, we're going to the Ministry. Shouldn't we look a little more respectable? I mean, prospective parents should play the part."

Roarke choked. "What in hell are you talking about?"

"Adopting Myune." She gave him a frank, defiant look.

Roarke grabbed Clover and held her close. He spoke gently to her, crooning in her ear.

"That's a very long shot. Clover, please don't set your heart on that. You'll get hurt." Roarke held her close, as if he could protect her from pain by keeping her pressed up against him.

"I know the problems. But that's what I want. Don't you?"

"It would be ideal. But life is not ideal. The government will take a dim view of our adopting a healthy, bright, Korean boy. They think of their boys and young men as national treasures. They would just as soon give you a piece of King Mud's jewelry as let you take Myune away."

Clover felt chilled by Roarke's pessimism. She wanted Myune as her own and prayed that Roarke would fight as hard as she would to get him.

"Please, Roarke. Don't you give up before we've even had a fair fight for him."

"I won't, you know that. But I don't want you hurt and I'm afraid that you'll have your heart broken. I know how deep your feelings go for people. You love Myune as if he really is yours. But, he isn't. He doesn't belong to anyone right now. Let's not tear him in two. We'll do what's best for him, not for us."

Clover cried. She couldn't think clearly. She wanted Roarke and Myune to herself. It was all she needed to live her life to the very fullest. Roarke had read her correctly. She did feel deeply about people she loved and she loved Roarke beyond all reason. If only their love could encompass a small, fragile little boy who had brought so much to their lives. If only . . .

As it turned out, Mrs. Kaeng and the farmer had no proof of their relationship to the boy and Clover felt that this was a sign that everything would finally come out all right.

Five weeks after they applied to the government to

adopt Myune, Clover was beginning to chafe at the delays. She and Roarke had asked the Reverend Cho to officiate at their marriage and he agreed. But, dear Lord, she fretted, can't it all be done quickly? The Reverend Cho failed to see any reason to hurry and had not set a date to marry them.

"I can't stand this uncertainty much longer," she complained to Jin-Soo in her office.

"You are always in such a hurry, Clover. You drive us all to distraction," Jin-Soo teased.

"You drive me up a mountain. How on earth do you ever get anything done?" she shouted back.

"What is it now, Clover?" Roarke walked into her office and sat down next to Jin-Soo, who had been relaxing in the monk's chair.

"East is East, Roarke," she grumbled.

"Clover is very impatient, as you know," Jin-Soo said.

"You can relax, doll. I cornered Reverend Cho and extracted a date for our wedding from him, with great difficulty, I might add," Roarke said.

"Congratulations, Roarke." Jin-Soo leaned over the chair and shook hands with Roarke.

Clover's face lit up. "When?" she asked.

"Next month at the Baptist Cathedral in downtown Seoul."

She clapped her hands and laughed. "Are you coming with me to see Myune today?" she asked. "I want to offer my help to Prince Yee. The palace is opening later this afternoon to show off the tomb finds."

Roarke smiled. "I doubt you'll have much of a crowd to contend with."

"I still want to assist, if I can. Come with me," she pleaded gently.

"Sure. You coming with us, Jin-Soo?" Roarke asked.

"Of course. This is a big day for me."

They drove together in silence. Roarke maneuvered

his car through the congested streets of Seoul only to come to a traffic jam near the palace that would shame the world's busiest cities.

"What in almighty is happening? Must be an accident." Roarke turned around and tried another approach without success. The streets had simply become gigantic parking lots around Prince Yee's palace. Roarke drove up onto a sidewalk and parked his car. "Let's walk," he said tersely.

Clover and Jin-Soo got out along with Roarke and pushed their way through a crowd of people reminiscent of a world soccer rally.

When they reached the palace, police were desperately trying to organize the people into lines, pushing and pulling them to and fro.

The crowd spotted Jin-Soo coming, and a roar went up.

Roarke was dumbstruck. "These people are here to see the tomb finds!"

"Yes. So they are," Clover answered.

They established their identity to the satisfaction of the police, and were able to enter the palace by a side door.

"Clover! Roarke! Did you see the people?" Myune shouted, and ran toward them.

"How could we help it?" Roarke answered, winking at Clover.

Myune grabbed Clover's hand and dragged her into a large room, where student workers were scurrying around covering the ancient wood floors with protective tarp.

"We are ready to let the people in." Prince Yee stood proudly among the precious finds from the tomb. "We will open the doors momentarily."

"I don't understand it," Roarke said.

"My dear Roarke. We are a people steeped in past traditions. It does not mean we cannot go forward into the future. It does mean we can always maintain our equilibrium by keeping our rich heritage alive. Love has many forms. We love our past. Let us keep it alive for our children and their children."

Roarke slowly walked around the room, looking into the display cases at the jewelry, pottery, glass jars, and dozens of other artifacts.

Clover beamed.

Prince Yee squeezed her hand. "You have many friends, Clover. More than you know. Myune is a fortunate boy."

Clover looked at him, startled. "What?"

Prince Yee nodded sagely. And Clover understood. Tears of joy streamed down her face as Myune told Roarke about each artifact while Roarke bent over to hear him, his hand on the boy's shoulder.

Epilogue

The strains of the wedding march echoed throughout the cavernous cathedral. The congregation stood and turned to watch Betty Witherspoon, Clover's matron of honor, glide slowly down the long aisle. At the front, Myune, a proud and solemn best man, peered around the pews to watch the procession; a hand reached out and gently pulled him back. Roarke grinned nervously. Before him the cathedral was crowded with well-wishers —friends and colleagues who had known him and Clover for a long time.

At last Clover appeared, a dazzling beauty in a long, soft-blue dress and wispy veil. Joy was so evident on her radiant face that the congregation nodded their approval. Her father beamed and accepted the fact that indeed his daughter was the most beautiful woman ever to walk down the bridal path.

Reverend Cho performed a short, lovely ceremony and pronounced them husband and wife. Only Clover knew that through the entire ceremony, Roarke was so nervous that he had difficulty slipping the ring on her finger. But now they were married and would go together to the next ceremony at the Changdok Palace prior to the reception in the palace's public gardens.

The weeks before the wedding, Clover had been busier than ever. But this time her reward was happiness, not exhaustion. Roarke had written his parents to tell them he was getting married to a woman he met in Korea, and adopting her son! They arrived in Seoul a few days after receiving the letter. His mother, as beautiful as Roarke had described her, feared she would never see her son again—that he would stay in his barracks with his M-1 gun.

The expression on her face was comical when she met Clover. She turned on Roarke angrily, stating that they had come to Korea so fast in order to spend time with their lost son. Clover assured them they would be back in the United States one day with Myune. Mrs. Devereaux took an immediate delight in the little boy and spent her time with him shopping and sightseeing.

Clover's parents arrived shortly before the wedding, and pronounced Roarke quite suitable for their only daughter. Feeling so complete with family and friends, Clover was indeed a happy woman.

"Sign here," Minister Hwang said. His brother Mr. Hwang, and the three hundred invited guests stood teary-eyed as Clover and Roarke signed the adoption papers in the palace throne room. Myune had been a perfect little boy during the marriage ceremony, not missing a beat as best man, including the moment when he dropped Clover's ring handing it to Roarke. He merely bent over, picked it up, and giggled. And now he stood next to Prince Yee as ramrod-straight as a soldier.

"Do we have to endure this party before we take off?" Roarke whispered in her ear.

"Shhh," she reprimanded gently.

After what seemed an endless round of toasts, cake, and dancing, Roarke grabbed Clover's arm firmly and ordered her to change into her street clothes.

"We have a plane to catch, remember?"

"I'll hurry." She kissed Myune for the one-hundredth time, kissed her mother and father and Roarke's parents, and finally broke away. Before they left the reception, Clover deliberately threw her bouquet to Betty, who blushed when she caught it.

Snuggled next to Roarke in a cab, she grinned when he said, "I plan to finish what we started in Hong Kong." Then he added, surprising her as only he could, "And maybe we'll finally have a brother or sister for Myune to play with? You know how much I love Myune, but there are some things a man likes to do for himself."

She nodded. A tear rolled down her cheek. She watched the moon rise over the east mountain. Did she imagine it, or did it really smile at her?

YOU'LL BE SWEPT AWAY WITH SILHOUETTE DESIRE

$1.75 each

1 ☐ James
2 ☐ Monet
3 ☐ Clay
4 ☐ Carey
5 ☐ Baker
6 ☐ Mallory
7 ☐ St. Claire
8 ☐ Dee
9 ☐ Simms
10 ☐ Smith

$1.95 each

11 ☐ James
12 ☐ Palmer
13 ☐ Wallace
14 ☐ Valley
15 ☐ Vernon
16 ☐ Major
17 ☐ Simms
18 ☐ Ross
19 ☐ James
20 ☐ Allison
21 ☐ Baker
22 ☐ Durant
23 ☐ Sunshine
24 ☐ Baxter
25 ☐ James
26 ☐ Palmer
27 ☐ Conrad
28 ☐ Lovan
29 ☐ Michelle
30 ☐ Lind
31 ☐ James
32 ☐ Clay
33 ☐ Powers
34 ☐ Milan
35 ☐ Major
36 ☐ Summers
37 ☐ James
38 ☐ Douglass
39 ☐ Monet
40 ☐ Mallory
41 ☐ St. Claire
42 ☐ Stewart
43 ☐ Simms
44 ☐ West
45 ☐ Clay
46 ☐ Chance
47 ☐ Michelle
48 ☐ Powers
49 ☐ James
50 ☐ Palmer
51 ☐ Lind
52 ☐ Morgan
53 ☐ Joyce
54 ☐ Fulford
55 ☐ James
56 ☐ Douglass
57 ☐ Michelle
58 ☐ Mallory
59 ☐ Powers
60 ☐ Dennis
61 ☐ Simms
62 ☐ Monet
63 ☐ Dee
64 ☐ Milan
65 ☐ Allison
66 ☐ Langtry
67 ☐ James
68 ☐ Browning
69 ☐ Carey
70 ☐ Victor
71 ☐ Joyce
72 ☐ Hart
73 ☐ St. Clair
74 ☐ Douglass
75 ☐ McKenna
76 ☐ Michelle
77 ☐ Lowell
78 ☐ Barber
79 ☐ Simms
80 ☐ Palmer
81 ☐ Kennedy
82 ☐ Clay
83 ☐ Chance
84 ☐ Powers
85 ☐ James
86 ☐ Malek

Coming Next Month

Nightwalker by Stephanie James

Cassie was alone in the old mansion when the lights went out—and she found Justin on her doorstep. Strange things began to happen . . . was Justin *really* her protector, or was Cassie fatally drawn to the instrument of her own destruction?

Take All Myself by Lucy Gordon

From the first Bryce Trafford and Beverly Darwin felt their love was inevitable. But Beverly was an actress in the volatile director's company—would the success they worked for together onstage end up driving them apart?

Too Near The Fire by Lindsay McKenna

Gil was the one man who'd ever touched the woman inside firefighter Leah Stevenson. Now he needed her to rescue two children, and only his love would bring her back out of the terrifying darkness and into the light.

Affairs Of State by Sara Fitzgerald

Maggie wasn't going to jeopardize her Senate seat for anything—but she hadn't counted on falling for reporter Robert Tate. She had to be wary of this man, but somehow politics wasn't on her mind when Robert took her in his arms!

Timeless Rituals by Laurel Evans

Archeologist Dana had long wished for a Viking to come out of the past and carry her off. All the same, she knew she should resist when her boss, Adam Nathan, became the modern day raider who was determined to steal her heart!

Rare Breed by Janet Joyce

Stacey knew she was more than reserved Jordan had bargained for—but she also knew that his cool manner was belied by the urgency in his green eyes. Would she ever be able to win his trust, as she was able to do with the wild animals she cared for?